THE DELIVERANCE OF CABO KOOB

ALEXANDER MALONE

NEWMAN SPRINGS PUBLISHING
320 Broad Street
Red Bank, NJ 07701

First originally published by Newman Springs Publishing 2020

Cover Photo taken by author, August 1969,
Nui Ba Den-Tay Ninh province, Vietnam

ISBN 978-1-64801-902-9 (Paperback)
ISBN 978-1-64801-903-6 (Digital)

Printed in the United States of America

PROLOGUE

Tay Ninh Province
South Vietnam
September 7, 1968

Major Sweeney's uniform had collected a fine layer of reddish-orange convoy dust during the open-jeep ride back to base camp. The major removed his armored vest and tossed it on the back seat of the jeep. After dismissing his driver, he then slapped briskly at the remaining loose dirt on his jacket and exposed forearms. He approached the colonel's office.

The building, a heavily-sandbagged prefab construction of lumber and screen wire, sat alone at the end of a raised walkway of wooden planks. The duck walk had been smartly lined on both sides with about four dozen brass casings, which had been scavenged from a nearby 155mm battery. The spent howitzer shells, now filled with sand to give them weight, stood upright—at attention, except for three. Two of those three had just recently been knocked over by a mischievous grunt, while his like-minded buddy, a celebrating short timer, had purposely stolen the third. The foolhardy GIs had willingly fell victim to both, the dare of last night's full moon, and the charity of too many free beers.

Maj. Herbert Sweeney, the Brigade S-2 officer, had been pressed to arrange this early briefing for his commanding officer and friend of many years, Col. Thomas Baird. He returned the salute of a passing soldier and then entered the colonel's office.

"Tom, I'm glad you're seated...and alone!" he began." Is that coffee I smell?" The two men shook hands. "We've got ourselves a helluva picture puzzle here, and wouldn't you know it…the most important pieces are missing from the box!"

The colonel cleared his throat, while reaching for the pot that held what remained of the coffee from earlier that morning. He poured a hot cup for the major. "Herb, I'm having a lousy week. Are you going to make it even worse?" He didn't expect a favorable answer.

"That's just very possible," the plain-speaking major responded. "Like I said before, it's a real puzzler? Let me tell ya' what I do know! At approximately 0700 hours this morning, a lone Caucasian with an RPG disabled one of Echo Company's armored tracks. He popped up from concealment and blew the APC's left track off cleanly with a single round. When the crew buttoned up to assess the threat, the carrier quickly filled with smoke from a fire they were unable to extinguish. Fearing that his own ordnance might start 'cooking-off' at any moment, the TC ordered everyone out. As they bailed out, this character got the drop on all four with an AK. He had 'em strip down to their underwear and then sent 'em packing on foot toward the village. They watched from a reasonable distance and then returned when they saw the fella leave, heading due south. Before he left, however, he took time to disable the APC's radio." He paused for a moment. "According to the driver, the only thing the guy took was third squad's medical kit. The kit had been assigned to this particular track."

The colonel sat silently, obviously moved by the incredible tale he had just heard. He cleared his throat and then spoke. "Caucasian, huh? Just how did the crew come to that conclusion?"

Major Sweeney then cleared his own throat. "Well, each member got a very good look at this character from up close, and they were pretty much unanimous in their description—blond hair, bearded, blue eyes, at least five feet, ten to eleven inches tall, approximately thirty to forty years old. He spoke a little English, at least enough to get that crew out of their clothes and walking down the road. He also mumbled something upon the entire crew, which they said sounded strangely like a curse, something about truth and how the crew deserved this fate because their fathers had killed his sister? I certainly don't know what to make of that. Oh yes! He was dressed like a local boy, right down to his black PJs, sandals, and sun bonnet."

The room grew very quiet, until Colonel Baird shouted out, "What the hell is a lone APC doing on that road at that time of day anyway?" He suspected that negligence and insubordination were factors that might very well have contributed to the circumstances leading up to the ambush, and he was certain that Sweeney would already know if his suspicions were justified.

The major cleared his throat a second time. "Three members of the track's regular crew and one other willing participant from commo were headed straight for the village in quest of true love… and, oh yes, some ice for their two cases of Budweiser. The crew knew the road had already been swept for mines, so they lied to the sentries at the gate. Said they needed to 'road test' a new fuel pump. They just kept on goin'!" Sweeney took his first and last sip of the colonel's coffee. "They're all on report and assigned to latrine duty at battalion until I personally say otherwise. I'm really disappointed because two of them boys earned a chest full of medals during Tet. But, by God, if there was a larger nastier latrine somewhere closer, then that's where I'd send 'em all! They've disgraced the entire troop. Article 15s are being drawn up for the enlisted men, but the track commander, a sergeant, will be court-martialed separately. It was his idea!

"Oh yes! There's one other interesting turn, which I'm sure you'll appreciate as much as I did. The TC and hitchhiker were not wearing any underwear when they were forced to undress, so a measure of justice has already been served!" They laughed, each obviously amused with that particular aspect of the unfolding mystery.

"So exactly what are we dealing with here, Herb? What do you think?"

Major Sweeney actually had several ideas. Since becoming aware of the ambush several hours ago, he had thought of little else. He moved to the window and looked out as an armored unit rumbled by. He waited until the noise subsided, then answered. "Tom, I think we can assume that this fella might be one of the following, an alienated GI, you know, a deserter with ideals, a political defector sympathetic to Uncle Ho's cause? On the other hand, he could very well be a Soviet advisor or technician. I haven't ruled out that he might be a hard-nut grunt who's gone completely loco. If it is a maverick GI, some information might be available in the regional MIA reports. We'll certainly look those over very carefully."

"One other consideration, whoever he is, he obviously knows how to disable a track. Believe me, I saw his work this morning, and it's better than most! His placement of that rocket could not have been sweeter. Lord knows he wasn't trying to destroy the track 'cause that would have been easy enough to do. Nope! This fella must have desperately wanted that medical bag because he did precisely what he needed to do to get it. The crew said that he didn't appear to be wounded or have any obvious physical problems. He looked healthy enough."

The colonel spoke again. "Maybe this spook isn't alone? Let's suppose that he's with someone who is wounded or someone who needs medical treatment, what exactly was in this particular aid kit?"

"Well, it had been replenished according to Echo Company's records, so it would have had six morphine syrettes,—each with the standard one-quarter grain dosage—two bottles of salt tablets, a bottle of alcohol, some aspirin, astringents, antiseptic ointment, vitamins, compress bandages, and gauze. The usual stuff. There was also a pair of scissors and a flashlight equipped with the standard red lens. That pretty much covers it. I know that drugs make people do some pretty crazy things, but I don't believe that this guy was just out looking for a fix of morphine. You and I both know how available heroin and opium are around here. Good God! That stuff is cheaper than the markdown price of a pair of used chopsticks. Nope, this fella wasn't after drugs. He was all business!"

Colonel Baird began to pace slowly around the small room. He paused at the rear door. "Well, hell! Since this guy is blowing up my tracks in my own backyard, then I guess we'll just have to meet for a little talk. Yep! That's exactly what we'll have to do." He looked at his watch for a moment. "Herb, this is what I want. For the next thirty-six hours, let's maintain laagers here, here, and here, with as many active dismounted patrols as each squadron can provide." He pointed to three locations on the wall map. The three points completely encompassed a broad area south and west of the ambush site. Sweeney carefully noted each position on the map. "Two nights is a long time to leave that armor just sitting around tempting Charley, so have them double their number of listening posts. I don't want any goofs or weed-heads fighting sleep all night in those LPs. By God, put some goddamn real Indians out there. Our spook's out there on foot, on the ground, the same as us. Let the tracks sit laagered out there two full nights to let this fellow know he's cornered, and there's no way out. He'll make a mistake and then we got 'em! If we don't kill him first, we'll have that little talk!"

"I'll get right on it," responded Major Sweeney. "I'll personally brief the field commanders." He turned to leave, then stopped short of the door. "Oh yeah, Tom! There is one more thing. Of all of our days spent together in this bog and the ditches of Korea, I gotta say your coffee today was the most frightening I've ever tasted!"

CHAPTER 1

Berlin, Germany
April 20, 1945

My name is Dieter Koob. My sister, Greta, and I were born of the same mother. Our time with our mother was brief as she chose to desert us while we were still very small. Greta always told me that our mother was ordered to leave us to serve in the Army Nursing Corps. Nurses are caring people. Greta wanted our mother to be a caring, loving person, and when she realized that she was not, she created the story for my benefit. We have different fathers, and they are unknown to us. I am big for my age and very strong. I do not need made-up stories to make me feel better inside.

I am fourteen years old, but will be fifteen later this month, on April 30. I was a good student until the invading Russian Army drew so near. When it became necessary to close the schools, many students with military training became soldiers. I love Berlin, and I am sad to see it being destroyed.

Spring slowly arrives, yet there are no birds to be heard singing. The air raids and continuous artillery bombardments have driven them out of the city. I wish I had wings to fly away with them. Greta has wings now. All angels have wings, and Greta is most certainly an angel.

My sister was a crewmember of a searchlight battery in Charlottenberg District. She was eighteen, and the only girl there with red hair and green eyes. She was teased frequently because of her beautiful red hair. Greta was killed in February during one of the nightly air raids.

She taught me many things, which I will always remember. She taught me the difference between a hard truth and a soft truth, explaining that an example of a hard truth would be a well-aimed rocket. This rocket, when delivered effectively, could destroy any Russian tank. Greta believed that dying for your beliefs was a soft truth. Greta died, as I might die, for someone else's beliefs. This makes her death a lie.

The bombs have killed many. Not even the wild animals in the zoo are spared. A rhinoceros and hyena lay dead in their cages, their bodies swollen by the warming sun. Some frightened but liberated monkeys cling to the highest branches of several trees just outside the gates of the zoo. They seem fearful of venturing any further. The recognizable stench of death is always present as bodies lay where they fall. Hordes of flies swarm everywhere. Many have turned their flower gardens and courtyards into gravesites for family and loved ones. I do not know where Greta rests.

The city is starving. Many Berliners have little to eat other than bits of stale bread and a few green carrots. Unspoiled potatoes are very difficult to find. The best food is confiscated first by the government officials and then the state police take that which is left. Water is available only if one can find a working hand pump. Milk for the children is unheard of. I wonder how the very little ones will survive if this iron siege continues much longer.

I am now a soldier of the German Guard. We are a collection of old men and boys who have been given the choice of fighting the Russian invaders or being publicly executed by the secret police. I have witnessed the bodies of those who refused hanging from lampposts. That is an ugly sight! Today is our Fuhrer's birthday!

*****

I am now fifteen, and I have personally destroyed three Russian tanks and their crews. The planes no longer fly over Berlin to drop their bombs as the Russian Army has entered the city from the south and the east. If the Amis and Englishers were to drop their bombs now, they would kill more Russians than Berliners. The Russians press forward from every front. I hear they are ferocious fighters, but I have yet to see a live one. Our defenses are not adequate and are crumbling rapidly. Berlin will soon be conquered.

The women of the city have a saying that is very appropriate for their situation. They yell to each other, "It is better to have a Russian on the belly than an Amis on the head!" This is their way of saying, "Better raped by the communists and left living than to be bombed by the Americans and left dead!" I have never seen a live American either, although there is an American that I like very much. His name is Tom Mix, the western cowboy. When I was eight, I saw a moving picture of his heroic feats at the theater. He has two gold teeth and a fine, smart horse named Tony. Tom's moving pictures have been forbidden for a long time because his mother was a Jew. I think he died while driving a big automobile through the American desert. I would like to have a gold tooth and drive a car. Tony is also dead.

My uniform consists of loose-fitting boots and a German cap. A helpful stranger encourages me to scavenge a steel helmet to protect my head at the first opportunity. I wear an Italian Army winter overcoat. The overcoat has three skillfully mended bullet holes in the front—one large hole, which penetrated the chest, and two smaller holes in the belly. I imagine that the Italian soldier was bravely facing his enemy when he was shot. I will be just as brave if my time comes.

The Russian tanks are large and noisy. They rumble blindly up the narrow streets where they become boxed in. The tanks then have no chance of reversing their direction. We have learned that is the best time to strike them. They are vulnerable to our rockets.

I destroyed the earlier tanks from a distance of forty meters. Some of the old men fire their rockets from as far away as two hundred meters. The weapons are useless at that distance, and they never hit their targets. I do not blame the older men for being afraid. I understand their wish to live. I do not want to die either!

*****

This is the first of May. The warmer weather brings with it an even greater awareness of death. My heavy overcoat is extremely hot and uncomfortable during the day, but it makes a fine warm blanket during the chill of night. The coat no longer has any buttons, so I have fashioned a sash for it with a length of wire.

The end is near for Berlin. Russian rockets scream as they are launched into the city for hours at a time. There is no escape from this terrifying sound. The Russian infantry now share the same ground with those of us who are left to fight. Several times, I have seen their cannons being pulled through the streets by teams of well-fed horses. The Russians are relentless in their attack. They leave us no time to dwell on our own hunger and misery.

CHAPTER 2

Several days have passed, and I am grateful to be alive. I am now a prisoner of the Russian Army. My capture, or worse yet, my death, seemed certain when considering the plight of my unit. After destroying two Russian tanks, we found ourselves outflanked on three sides. A third tank appeared at my front. As I reached for a new launcher, the tank fired its cannon. Unfortunately for me, the shell struck the building that I had huddled against for protection. The explosion brought the bricks of the wall quickly down on top of me, burying my body, with only my legs visible from the street.

I must have been rendered unconscious from the blast. As I slowly recovered my senses, I also became aware of strong hands pulling at my ankles. I heard the voices of Russian soldiers who were tossing away the loose bricks. Once I had been uncovered from the rubble, the soldiers methodically scoured my body from head to feet. They were hoping to find a watch on my dead body, but I had nothing of value. I received a sudden blow to the head as a gesture of their disappointment. Their commander was nearby.

I was startled by the youthful appearance of their leader. He was very young, perhaps, but just a few years older than myself. He approached where I lay shaken from the explosion. He stopped and then gave one of the men of his command an order to pour some water on my head. The soldier opened his canteen and did as ordered. The young officer then signaled for another soldier, an interpreter, to join him. Through his interpreter, the young commander denounced me for being a stooge of the Fascists. I sensed that it would be useless to deny this accusation, so I remained silent. The interpreter then began to boast of the exploits of his great commander. Through this interpreter, I learned the young commander had received decorations for bravery in battle and rewarded with an officer's commission. The young Russian officer obviously enjoyed hearing the tales of his heroic deeds being translated into German. When they had finished with me, I was taken behind their lines to be processed as a prisoner of war.

*****

I observed the end of the war as a prisoner of the Soviets. Today, we are commanded to help the Russians dispose of many bodies from the battle. We drag the bodies of the fallen into the street, where they are stacked like pieces of wood. Russian soldiers incinerate the remains by torching them with flamethrowers. One must turn away from this sight or be sickened by it!

Our Russian guards are starving us. I am so hungry! If the war is over, why are we still being held captive? Many men are smoking cigarettes fashioned from cheap Russian tobacco. They say that this helps to relieve the agony of their terrible hunger.

*****

This week, we are being transported by freight train to a prisoner-of-war camp somewhere in eastern Poland. The freight car sways back and forth and from side to side. We have been packed into this car so tightly that those who have died cannot fall. If these deaths are reported to the guards, then our meager ration of food will be decreased even more.

The Christians among these dead are forbidden from having any burial rites. Our guards say that German prisoners will be used to rebuild all of the Russian cities destroyed by Germany.

*****

Winter has arrived, and I am in a prison labor camp. It is a very bad place. Many of the guards are extremely brutal when plied with vodka. It is very cold outside and not much warmer inside the thin-walled wooden barracks where we live. I overhear some of the prisoners jokingly remark that it is best not to be too warm anyway as that warmth would attract even more lice to your body. We survive on a watery cabbage-and-potato soup. Some days, we receive a piece of black bread with a lump of sugar. We are deloused occasionally, but the lice always return.

I am wearing the uniform that I was captured in over seven months ago, but the guards have taken the piece of wire that I had used for a belt. Fleas and lice live comfortably in the clothes with me also.

We work fourteen to eighteen hours a day. Sometimes, our own countrymen supervise us during work. These are men who have betrayed us to get better rations for themselves. There is a general rule in the labor camp. If one does not work, one does not eat! This is a hard truth. The work involves chopping down trees, clearing land, and cutting the wood into firewood. Very little of the firewood is for our use. It is stacked beside the railroad lines for distribution to the occupying Russian Army. Many men have contracted tuberculosis since arriving here. I am thankful for my health.

*****

It is now December, and I have been told that I will be released soon with others as part of a prisoner exchange between the Allies and Russia. German prisoners of war are being swapped for Russian citizens who defected when Stalin took control. I do not envy these people as they will certainly be treated as badly as we were. I cannot dwell on these unfortunate people as our own hardships have been severe enough.

There is much happiness and cause for celebration in the barracks. Even those who are not being released are excited for those of us who are. They have finally been given a reason to continue on.

There is evidence now to support the rumors. Presentable clothing has arrived, along with footwear and soap!

*****

My group has traveled by train from Poland to Leipzig, Germany. On this journey, I have not looked away from the destruction of the war. There is sadness and sorrow on the faces of my countrymen everywhere. Rubble and ruins lie where great stone buildings once stood. Germany has been destroyed!

In Leipzig, we are transferred to a large POW camp that was built to accommodate our large numbers. We are glad to finally be released from the Russians. The allied armies of the West are responsible for the operation of this new camp, and the conditions here are much improved. Our spirits are renewed by the unexpected tolerance of our new captors.

It has taken eighteen days for the Allies to process the documents of our release. I am now free to leave but unsure of where to go. Home? The city of Berlin is in total ruin. A landscape of doom extends in every direction. It would be a difficult challenge to survive there. Two trustworthy comrades have agreed to let me accompany them until our fortunes improve.

I have known Otto Bak as my friend for many months. He prefers being known as Blackie. Blackie is very smart. He was a teacher in Bonn before the war. He is unmarried and has not spoken of a family. Prior to his capture in Berlin, Blackie held the rank of sergent. He always said that life in the Russian camps was agreeable with him because there was no women's cooking there. He says that he does not like for women to cook, but I do not ask why.

It was Blackie who approached me the first night of our captivity together back in May. He said that he held a secret that the Russians would be pleased to learn of, and to prevent that from happening, he needed the help of a fellow prisoner. After I had sworn to an oath of personal secrecy, Blackie cautiously unbuttoned his heavy winter overcoat and the blouse underneath. He slowly raised his left arm, but only after determining that no guards were looking in our direction. There, just beneath the armpit, was revealed a small tattoo of two lightning bolts, identical in every feature. A number was clearly visible below the lightning bolts. After I had taken a look at the tattoo, Blackie casually lowered his arm and secured his clothing. He confided that he was a doomed man because of the tattoo. It marked him, as well as others of his former unit, for certain death. The Russians would eventually discover the tattoo and then execute him immediately afterward. I did not ask why.

Blackie had a plan for removing the incriminating tattoo. He said that he needed to place a glowing hot ember from the cooking fire directly over the tattoo. The heat would scar the skin tissue, enough to make the tattoo unrecognizable. Because of my youth, Blackie assumed that the guards would ignore me. I could retrieve the hot coal that would be needed, if he were to survive Russian captivity. I agreed to help, and although his pain was extreme that night, Blackie's plan worked perfectly. We are now friends. I am pleased that my friend has a gold tooth like Tom Mix.

My adopted guardian is Guenther Dern. Guenther is a master printer at a large shop in Cologne. He is smart as well. He has served in army campaigns in Italy and Poland. We first met at the prison labor camp in Poland. He is married and has a young son. Perhaps that is why he thinks that he must look after me? Guenther has not heard from his family for over a year prior to his capture. He seldom speaks of them, but I know he worries constantly for their safety.

*****

The three of us have decided to travel together to Cologne, but it is unlikely that we will reach there before Christmas. We lack money to buy food, and yet we do not beg or rob. There are kind people everywhere. These kind people have very little, and yet they willing provide bits of food to passing strangers. We are humbled by the generosity of our countrymen.

This morning, we have reached Cologne, and here, before us, lies a scene of incredible horror. Firebombs have rendered this beautiful city into ash and cinder. Only the city's cathedral remains standing, high above the roofless, gutted shells of neighboring buildings. A nearby bridge has collapsed into the river, and there are no other bridges in sight. Guenther is frustrated. There are no other recognizable features to the city. I understand his frustration. Many of the streets are closed to traffic. These remain filled with rubble from the collapsed buildings. I fear his family has perished as few could have survived the experience of this hell. And it was surely that! We encounter laborers pushing carts of rubbish out of the streets. These survivors tell us that thousands of people died in one single night of firebombing.

We will remain here as long as Guenther wishes. We will assist him in trying to locate his family for we are certain that he would do the same for us. At our makeshift camp tonight amid the rubble of Cologne, Blackie and I lack words sufficient to comfort our friend. It is a cold, cold Christmas Eve.

It is early morning, and work details are already clearing rubble from the streets. We hear the Allies have teams that have been searching for missing persons. Perhaps, they can help us? The Allies are keeping records of displaced people in the city. Maybe they will let us look at their records. We must go to the Allied command center.

The Allied compound is easy to find. Once there, we are quickly directed to a unit known as Graves Registration. Our search ends here. The names of Guenther's wife and son are found listed in a journal of those confirmed as dead. The dates of their deaths are also recorded in the journal. Guenther Dern, a strong man and veteran of five tearless years of brutal war, weeps softly. Blackie stands silently, looking out over the ruins of the city.

CHAPTER 3

Today marks the beginning of a new year…1946. Our uncertain futures look brighter today as the result of an encounter with a much-traveled character. He claims that enlistment in the French Foreign Legion has become the honorable quest for many displaced veterans. The stranger says he knows of many comrades who have traveled to Marseilles, France, to enlist.

The stranger, who identifies himself only as Kurt, is a peculiar man. He is anxious to share this good news with anyone who will listen. We do listen as he tells of the French struggle to rebuild an army that was decimated by the war. The country now has very few citizens of military age. Blackie reminds us that France is recovering from the loss of six million men in the first big war twenty-five years earlier.

This fellow, Kurt, is a fountain of information. He says that the ranks of the Legion are filled with fervent anticommunists. Citizens of France are not allowed to join the Legion. They are required to join the regular French Army. He says that Legion officers are mainly French, however.

Kurt explains that those accepted into the Legion are paid a monthly wage of 400 French francs. They also receive an enlistment bonus of 500 francs with their first month's pay. The food is rumored to be very good, and legionnaires can expect, at least, one satisfying meal every day. A sum equaling 900 French francs! That sounds like a lot! I must learn the value of money!

I blink nervously when he says that enlistees must stand at least five feet and two inches tall and be at least eighteen years of age. Also, one must be of good health in general. The stranger says not to be concerned with papers or documents because no verifications are requested. Birth certificates, passports and identification papers are unnecessary. Those seeking to enlist are not asked to present any documentation of any type, but they can expect to be subjected to a personal interrogation by the Legion recruiters.

I will be sixteen years old in two months, so I must somehow make the recruiters believe that I am eighteen. If I could grow a beard of scruff like Blackie, I would look much older. But that is impossible. Guenther remains confident that I can fool the interrogators into believing that I am older. As I stand five feet and eight inches already, I should have to deceive no one of that fact!

We are roused by this unique chance to escape from the hopelessness around us. A new start with wages and regular meals! Tonight, around our campfire, we discuss the matter further. This could be a great opportunity for each of us. Our voices are filled with renewed spirit as we each agree to cast our lot with the French Legion! Now that it has been decided, we immediately begin to plan our journey through France. I overhear Blackie remark how the Legion will be perfect for him because he does not care for food that has been prepared by women. Again, I am confused. Perhaps he is merely having a joke with us? One day, I will ask him to explain his words.

We reach Dijon, France, by successfully stowing away on the few trains that are available to us. Trucks occasionally reduce their speeds enough for us to climb aboard. Good fortune rides with us as we cover great distances. Soon, we reach the city of Lyon. After resting here for one day, we discover a coal train destined for return to Marseilles. We steal aboard the train unseen and arrive at the busy port city three days later. The city is thriving and seemingly untouched by the war.

After receiving directions from helpful strangers, we have no difficulty finding the Legion's recruiting depot. We pause momentarily to celebrate the completion of a successful journey. I eagerly study the very place that has been in our dreams for so many days. The depot is an old stone fortress that once defended the port of Marseilles from invaders. The tricolors of the French Flag are now flying high above the entrance gate of the ancient fort.

Several dozen haggard men are seen milling aimlessly around the base of the flag. Others appear to be resting on the dusty street corner. Their dirty, rumpled clothing easily identifies them to be unemployed transients like we. Many of the men are old and appear to be of poor health. Some are younger. Regardless of age, each man's face reflects an unvarying image of lost hope. We learn that these unfortunate souls were rejected by the Legion several days earlier, and they have nowhere else to go. I have known for some time now that life is not always sweet. It comes with fateful measures of bitterness as well. A regular dose of bitter fruit can render a man unworthy in his own eyes. It will ruin him! I fear that this depot is the final hope for these frail, ragged, hungry men. Their lives of desperation will continue.

My comrades and I wish each other good luck as we enter the recruiting station. "Stand straight like a man, like the soldier you are! Posture is important!" encourages Guenther.

"Yes, and look directly into the Frenchmen's eyes when they interrogate you," adds Blackie. "You may just fool them!"

Those who do not understand the French language are separated from those who do. Then we are divided into smaller groups, where I overhear both French and German being spoken. I am hastily directed to a small room occupied by a lone legionnaire who is seated behind a large desk. He is dressed in a uniform of a khaki blouse and green necktie. His trousers are also khaki, and on his head, he wears a strange white cap. There are several military decorations pinned to the legionnaire's blouse. He stares curiously at me at first, saying nothing. Suddenly, he begins to read from a list of questions. I answer...

"My name is Dieter Koob."

"Yes, I am eighteen years of age."

"My birthday is April 30, 1927."

"Yes, I will be nineteen in two months."

"Yes, I am five feet and eight or more inches."

"No, I do not have a birth certificate."

"No, I do not have a passport."

"No, I do not have tuberculosis."

"Yes, I fought in the defense of the Fatherland."

"No, Communism must be destroyed."

"No, I do not need twenty-four hours to think about my decision to enlist in the Legion."

At this point, the recruiter informs me that I will have to wait twenty-four hours like everyone else because that time is necessary to develop the X-ray picture of my lungs. Seemingly satisfied with my interrogation thus far, he accompanies me to the medical examination room and leaves me there in the presence of a medical doctor.

The doctor also asks if I have tuberculosis and when I reply no to this, he directs me into a small closet where an X-ray picture is taken of my chest. The experience is painless. I am weighed, and my height is verified. He feels my pulse. Next, the doctor taps my chest and back and then records his findings in a logbook. The same interrogator appears and escorts me from this office. As we walk, he remarks that he remembers my birthday because it is the same date as the Day of Camerone. He adds that all new recruits will soon become familiar with the greatest day in Legion history!

He orders me to be back here tomorrow morning at eight o'clock for further instructions. I am one day closer to becoming a legionnaire. It seems my date of birth is of more importance to the Legion than my age itself. Guenther and Blackie find this lucky coincidence to be very favorable for my cause. Greta would find it to be another soft truth.

Two days have now passed, and the three of us are very excited. Guenther, Blackie and I are being welcomed into the Legion with a short speech and our first complete meal in years. Not everyone here has reason to be joyous as a full score of men has been rejected. Some of the poor men still remain outside near the main gate.

Upon receiving our good news, we are instructed to form ranks to take an oath of allegiance to France and the French government. Solemnly, I recite the oath, aware that my heart and true allegiance are with Germany. When the French officer has completed administering the oath, he proudly proclaims "Legion Patria Nostra," which means "The Legion Is Our Fatherland." He states that we are now subjects of France and must obey all laws and regulations of the French government.

It is obvious to the Legion cadre that we are very hungry and must be fed soon. In a very short time, we are marched into a huge room filled with long rows of benches and tables. At first, I am startled by the incredible height of the dining hall's ceiling. We are commanded to sit for our very first *soupe*. My friends and I are suddenly disappointed at the mention of soupe. I remember well the horrible soupe that kept us alive in the prison labor camps. Maybe, the Legion soupe will be sufficient for our present needs? We shall see. As we are waiting for our soupe to be brought from the kitchen, we are informed that every meal in the Legion is referred to as soupe. It is an Arabic expression that was assumed by the Legion many years ago.

We are soon served large mugs of hot black coffee, thick chunks of gray bread, and macaroni stew with meat in it. The clanking sounds of metal spoons striking metal trays fill the room of happy men. Is hope being restored…or will we awake from this dream to find ourselves still weak from hunger? No! This is no dream. In my dreams, the food is never this good!

Our tables are well tended to, and we soon have our fill of satisfying food. At this time, we are given more information from the Legion cadres. They explain the simple details of our contract with France, which must be honored for five years. That does not seem like a long time. We are told that if we remain with the Legion for fifteen years, we will receive a pension—and French citizenship. Our enlistment bonus will be 500 French francs, just as Kurt had promised. We will also receive a daily wage of twelve francs! We are told that uniforms will not be issued until we reach Sidi Bel Abbes. That is the name of the town in Algeria where the French Foreign Legion has its home. A map in the fortress hallway clearly shows Sidi Bel Abbes in North Africa, in the country of Algeria. We are then issued tickets that will be used for train passage once we reach North Africa. FRENCH LEGION is printed in black letters on each ticket. I clutch mine tightly, knowing that if I should lose it, I may not be issued another. Satisfied from the meal and with our spirits soaring, we are dismissed after a stern warning of the consequences for missing roll call in the morning. We are to be at the docks at dawn to begin our voyage to Africa.

We decide to camp in a public courtyard. From here, it will be a quick walk to the docks. Our boat is already there, waiting for us. I am too excited to sleep tonight! Tomorrow will be here soon. Guenther says he was transported by ship during his service in Italy. Blackie has traveled on a steamship, but he is sleepy now and does not wish to talk.

This morning, we arrive at the docks early to discover that we are not the first ones here. Hordes of other determined men have arrived early. No one can afford to be left behind. The kitchen staff provides us with an early fare of strong black coffee, cheese and more of the gray army bread. We take our fill. The strong coffee has become cold, but it continues to satisfy our need.

We have located our ship. It, or she, as boats are always considered female, flies the flag of Belgium and is named *Lausanne*. She is an old, old ship. It is remarkable that she is still afloat and not resting quietly on the harbor bottom. Presently without cargo, she sits high in the water, embarrassed, unable to hide her many imperfections. Her rusting nakedness is visible to everyone. Blister bubbles have developed under her many layers of cheap paint. But regardless of her appearance, I trust that she is still worthy enough to deliver us to our new lives.

When the last crumbs of cheese and bread are gone, the cadres quickly organize us into two columns, and we board *Lausanne*.

We are escorted below several decks and separated into groups of exactly forty men. There are two signs bolted to the steel walls of our compartment. One reads: "Eight horses or forty men." The other sign reads in French: "*huit chevaux-quarante hommes.*" Judging from the size of this area, neither horse nor man is blessed with any advantage in comfort. This small confine reminds me of how grateful I am to no longer be held captive. If we are given any freedom of movement, I will go up on deck where I can see the sky. Maybe unwashed bodies and soiled clothing have not fouled the air up there. I may smell worse than anyone else on board this ship.

After three days and two nights at sea, our voyage ends as *Lausanne* docks this afternoon in the port city of Oran, Algeria. From the pier, we march as a group to the train depot.

There is a delay of several hours while our train is readied for the journey to the city of Sidi Bel Abbes. After a hastily served ration of sausages, black bread, and warm coffee, we board train cars that, once again, are obviously intended and designed for hauling cattle.

Again, as on board *Lausanne*, we have been organized into groups of forty men, and again signs are there to remind the loaders: "eight horses or forty men." There are benches for those who wish to sit, but most of us prefer to stand and stare out at this new strange countryside as we slowly chug through it. The eighty kilometers by rail is tiring and takes over six hours, but we finally arrive. Although everyone is tiring, I am alert and truly excited to be a new traveler on the mysterious continent of Africa.

Upon arrival in Sidi Bel Abbes, we are met by a detail of legionnaires in uniforms, which are identical to those of the recruiters in Marseilles. They also wear the strange white caps. Their mission is to escort us from the rail depot to the Legion compound. Each member of our escort carries a rifle and wears a knapsack and cartridge belt. I will certainly look smart in this uniform when my training is completed.

We are loosely assembled into a formation of poorly dressed men to complete our journey to the Legion compound. Our march takes us through the very center of the town. Many townspeople line the street as we pass. Others begin to slowly emerge from their homes and shops to gawk at our pitiful condition. Some offer remarks that only they can laugh at. They are obviously unimpressed with our appearance. Along the march, small children begin to follow. Other children yell insults while peering out from behind their parents.

Loud barking dogs wander everywhere. A few members of our Legion escort carry stones in the pockets of their uniforms. They have come prepared to deal with the barking mongrels. A barrage of well-thrown rocks has the cowardly dogs yelping and scurrying for cover.

A short time later, we march through the gates under the impressive arch of the Legion Headquarters. We enter onto a large parade field, and the order to halt is given. We are instructed to stand silently in our ranks, facing a white wooden platform. An impressive hedge of neatly trimmed green shrubbery grows around the freshly painted platform.

After a brief wait, a sergent-major from the Legion Headquarters appears and climbs the steps of the platform. I am impressed with his appearance. He wears the same uniform as our Legion escort, but instead of the green tie, his neck is wrapped with a white scarf. He wears the same strange headgear, which we have been told is called a *kepi blanc*. We learn that we will receive one only after we have successfully completed our training here.

I listen closely to the words of the sergent-major as he speaks into an electric microphone. First, he addresses us in French. I understand very little. I am not the only person who fails to understand what he is saying. After a brief pause, the sergent-major surprises each of us by delivering the same message in German. This seems logical since most of us are German. We foolishly realize that the sergent-major is also German!

The words of the sergent-major follow. "Legio Patria Nostra! Welcome to Sidi Bel Abbes. Here, you will train hard to become soldiers of Le Legion d'Etranger. The glorious Legion will become your home. The Legion will feed you. The Legion will clothe you. And the Legion will nurse your many wounds. If you should die while wearing the beloved uniform of my Legion, you will have died well, because dying well for the Legion is far better than living badly.

"You will train hard and you will fight hard. You will do this for France, the mother of our dear Legion. Your training will be very difficult, and no thoughts or acts of desertion will be tolerated. Punishment for any violation is severe, whether it is for dereliction of duty, disobedience, or that of a criminal nature. I repeat, most severe!

"This should be ample warning for those of you who have the stubborn nature of the mule and do not willingly follow the orders of your superiors. We will take your spirit and crush it until there is nothing left and then rebuild it anew using the mold of the Legionnaire.

Heaven help you if you should not fit into this mold. Listen very carefully to your superiors. For those of you who do not speak French or German, there is still hope of success. *Faites comme moi,* or do as I do, and you will prevail without suffering unnecessarily!"

After this magnificent speech, we are divided into squads for our training and assigned noncommissioned officers as cadres to supervise us. These are referred to as NCOs. Two of the elderly NCOs are corporals, but they insist on being addressed only as *cabos.*

We are fed, and then we march to our barrack to rest until reveille the next morning. The barrack is clean, and everyone has their own bed, with a wooden shelf on the wall just over the bed. An empty rack for rifles is affixed to the wall nearest the entrance. The Legion is now both my home and my school.

CHAPTER 4

Reveille, 0530. I rise from a night of sound, restful sleep. After soupe of coffee, more of the French Army bread, sardines. and cheese, our squad marches to the supply warehouse. Here, we are issued uniforms that identify us as recruits and not real legionnaires. These training uniforms are ill-matched, ill-fitting remnants of other various Legion outfits. Some are non-Legion altogether. There are trousers from both the American and British armies. The blouses come from Spain and Greece. However, our assortment of boots and shoes is remarkably similar, being either black or dark brown in color. We are issued leather belts, knapsacks, and mess tins. These mess kits will be used for all meals when we are training in the field. We are given cartridge belts but no cartridges or rifles.

We dress hurriedly, carefully saving our old civilian clothes by wrapping them in old newspaper. We have been informed by one of the corporals that the local merchants will buy these clothes for a few francs regardless of their condition. I have been wearing the very same clothes that were issued prior to my release from Russian captivity.

We march to the infirmary for a new round of physical examinations. Every man receives a single inoculation in the back. It is a quick stab between the shoulder blades. These shots are very powerful. We receive a warning to expect of reaction of high fever and soreness of body for at least two days. For these reasons, we march back to our barracks where we will be confined for 48 hours. All activities are cancelled, and our barracks is placed under quarantine.

It is the second day of the quarantine, and I have not reacted to the inoculation. Blackie has a temperature of 104 degrees, and he begs for me to end his suffering with a bullet. I remind him that we have received neither weapons nor bullets yet, so he will have to continue suffering. Guenther is assigned to another barrack, so I do not know if he became ill. He warned me earlier to choose my companions carefully in this place. Following this sound advice, I respond by keeping a cautionary distance from the other members of my squad.

I welcome the third day after the shots, and still, I have had no reaction. I am fortunate as I witness the misery of those around me. Today, Blackie and many of the sick will attempt to keep their food down. One legionnaire, Cabo Andersen, has gathered our packages of old clothing. The old corporal is taking our dirty ragged clothes into the town where he will sell them to the merchants. Based on what he tells us, I expect to receive either four or five francs in return. He startles us by revealing that the merchants will clean and make repairs to our old clothes and then they will sell them back to deserting legionnaires at extremely higher prices.

Cabo Andersen is a fine man, but a terrible foul stench hovers around him constantly. It is rumored that he has never taken a bath. It is also humorously rumored that his offensive odor was the true cause of the redness in the sick men's eyes. His uniform is remarkably clean, and I might add that he looks magnificent in it, but he smells like rotting garbage!

Cabo Andersen is older than any of the other cadres and says he actually fought against a tribe of warriors called the Berbers. He tells us that he was born in Scandia, a part of Sweden, but swears of knowing of no other life outside of the Legion. He encourages us to visit the post library as well as the Legion museum, with its vast collection of historic relics. I will do this once the quarantine is removed.

The corporal, or cabo, as the older NCOs prefer to be addressed, states that I appear to be the youngest member of the entire company. If that's true, then I will be given the honor of reading the sacred account of the Battle of the Camerone. It is traditional for this reading to fall upon the youngest member every year on April 30. Cabo Andersen says that this heroic engagement in Mexico is viewed as the most glorious day of battle in the history of the French Foreign Legion. The Day of Camerone is the largest celebration of the year for legionnaires, regardless of where one might be stationed.

A day of requiem…a day of light duty…and a day of wine, music, and revelry!

*****

Reveille 0530
Soupe
Drill until 1000
Soupe
Drill until 1730
Soupe
Prepare for inspection
Sleep

Everyone's health has returned from wherever it has been. A training schedule is presented to us today, our fifth day. The cadres follow it very strictly! The leader is Sergent-Chef Wimmer. He warns us of the importance of the training schedule displayed at the entrance to the barracks. He cautions us to study it carefully each morning because a duty roster will be posted there every day also. Harsh discipline will be the consequence for any missed assignment.

We march in groups at all times, and no movement is allowed outside the barracks unless one has orders. We must stand at attention when eating in the central dining hall. Sergent Wimmer will judge our progress in training and will allow us to sit only after he determines that our progress is satisfactory. Rifles will be issued tomorrow!

It is the third week here, and a busy first day as denoted by the duty roster.

No. 494321 Kitchen detail 0400–2230

Each of us has been assigned a personal number that we commit to memory. Number 494321 has been assigned to me, Trainee Dieter Koob. No recruit is ever referred to by the name that he enlisted under, regardless of whether that name is real or merely an alias. In truth, many are aliases! Names will be used only after graduation.

30

Recruits are even allowed to assume another name if they wish but, still, only after graduation.

The food is always satisfying. During my previous assignments to the pantry, I was impressed by the care and preparation that went into every meal. The scene in the gigantic kitchen is an occasion of wonder. The cooks, some of whom are actual chefs, are an active collection of men from all over. They seldom speak to those around them and then only if there is an unexpected emergency in the preparation of soupe. Beginning today, we may sit during meals!

Blackie as well as Guenther, whom I often see from a distance, are now clean shaven. Each has been issued a shaving kit from the commissary. I have yet to speak with Guenther, but he appears to be content. Cabo Andersen's unwashed body still screams, but alas, because of his rank, not one of us is man enough to dare tell him. Only one legionnaire refers to me as "chapeau" when my work pleases him, and that is Cabo Andersen! He says to me, "I don't have any brains or religion, so that makes me someone you can trust!"

I have become familiar with the call of the trumpet. We rise each morning to face another day of extreme challenges. Our bodies are being conditioned to endure the heat of the route marches in the hot African sun. The length of these marches increased from ten miles during our second week to thirty miles our fourth week. At first, these exercises were in an area of very flat terrain. Today, however, we march off of the usual trail into the hill country. Thorny desert bushes block our path. The brambles become so thick that we are forced to hack a passage through it with our machetes. Soon, many of us realize that we have carelessly exhausted the water in our canteens. My pack is heavy. In addition to the full musset and rifle, each of us is required to carry two pieces of firewood for the cooking fires. This wood is needed for the preparation of food when we march. Fortunately for us, the pack mules at the rear of our column are burdened with the actual foodstuffs and cooking wares.

We continue marching without water or relief from the oppressive heat. Squad members falter, lacking strength to keep pace. I trudge onward, being careful not to stumble over the weaker men who have collapsed in my path. The fallen men lie exhausted on the hot sands, their legs locked tight in wretched pain, unable to take even one more step. There is enough suffering for everyone. Even the pack mules seem to be languishing on this particular day. I, too, have taken the last of my water, and now my lips and tongue are beginning to swell from the dryness. The sergent in command of today's march refuses to allow anyone to share their remaining water with those who have none. Because of this, many suffer. No one speaks, however, except for an occasional curse aimed directly at the sergent. Only a cruel man with absolute power could deprive thirsting men of water. Maybe the sergent must be cruel if his students are stubborn oafs and can learn only in this manner.

This is my school, and I have taken a vow to study each lesson well. On this day, I learn that water is vital to life itself in an unforgiving climate. We are forced to practice conservation because our canteen water must also be shared with the cooks, otherwise, there would be no food while in the field. I sense that we are being prepared to face all challenges as a unit, not as individuals. I sense that survival for life itself may someday require such unity, cooperation and discipline.

*****

Rifles are issued to each man this week. This is an exciting time. For what is a soldier without the means to defend himself and his comrades? My assigned rifle is made in France. It is designed to fire only one bullet at a time. To do this, I slide the bolt back to uncover or open the breech. Then a single cartridge is loaded into the breech by sliding the bolt forward as far as it will go. My rifle is then ready to fire.

During marksmanship training, we are given loose rounds that we carry in our cartridge belts. I am informed that ammunition is in short supply for the Legion. It must also be rationed like our water. We are drilled repeatedly on the care and cleaning of our rifles, and after many lessons, I graduate as a qualified rifleman.

We are also learning to march in close ranks with our rifles and to properly execute the manual of arms. These drills are necessary to keep us from accidentally striking those nearest us when we are standing in the close formations or marching as a body. The arms drills prove to be very difficult, and our NCOs constantly berate the slowest learners in the unit.

They work to teach us the techniques needed for mastering commands such as: Present Arms, Shoulder Arms, Port Arms, Inspection Arms, and Ready Arms. We know that we will not graduate as a body until each of us can perform these drills first as individuals.

Not everyone here progresses well. Local trackers have apprehended and returned two deserters from our barracks. The culprits presently await their fate in the stockade.

Blackie had warned me earlier to avoid both men, stating only that they were untrustworthy. The punishment for the deserters will be administered quickly. Cabo Andersen tells us that the two men are of no use to anyone while they are locked away, so they will rejoin us soon.

Blackie and I have many opportunities to talk, but he rarely speaks of his earlier life, or the war. He will only say that he fought the Russians for three years. Peace does not come easily for veterans of the war. The horrors of a long desperate struggle for survival are still fresh in their minds. Some have regrets. All have memories. Neither will ever fade completely from their minds. This is a good place for Blackie. A busy life is good tonic for my troubled friend.

We wash, mend, sew, iron, clean, mop, polish, sweep, scrub, and repair when we are not engaged in our lessons. That is the only way to keep up with the demands of our training. I understand why there will be no passes issued until after graduation. There is simply no time to relax.

Noncommissioned Officer Fulci's wife is a prostitute at a city brothel. He actively encourages the men here in the barracks to visit her whenever they have the opportunity. Cabo Fulci does not seem concerned that his wife earns her living as a prostitute. They work as one in the true spirit of matrimony. She saves a substantial portion of her earnings, while he accumulates time toward his Legion pension. Fulci declares that they wish to retire very soon. Jokingly, he adds that she is more eager to retire than he is!

Even as training continues, we receive a daily ration of wine, equal to one-fourth liter. The cadres carefully measure this serving, which amounts to only a few generous swallows. A single ration is not enough to induce intoxication; however, many become drunk after purchasing the allotments of others.

With Cabo Andersen's permission, I visit the museum. On the way, I stop to behold the most prominent Legion Monument to the Dead. This impressive monument is a giant metal globe of earth sitting atop a stone pedestal. It is inscribed with the words "*Honneur et Fidelite.*" There is a single gold star, strategically displayed on the globe in the country of Mexico. I stand here in awe for some time and then continue my walk to the museum.

There are many interesting artifacts from the Legion's history on display here—flags, uniforms, swords and other weapons, but the most unusual item is a wooden hand in a glass case. An inscription on the base of the exhibit identifies the artificial hand's owner as Major Danjou, a famous Legion commander killed at Camerone, Mexico, in 1863. Now I understand why the gold star on the Legion monument is in Mexico. I anticipate this special day when I shall read the story of Camerone to Guenther, Blackie, and the other legionnaires. My visit to the museum is brief, and I do not have enough time to see everything. I will return again soon—with permission, of course.

CHAPTER 5

Algeria is a strange land. In Sidi Bel Abbes, there are more dogs than camels. The miserable hounds run freely through our living quarters, stopping often to scratch at their busy flea friends. Cabo Fulci swears that when one becomes accustomed to the smell of the camel, then that person's nose has been in Algeria too long. If he finds the odor of the camel to be offensive, how then can he tolerate the stench of a certain corporal? The camels are strange animals, indeed, but their smell is like sweet perfume when compared to that of Cabo Andersen.

Today, I am ordered to the post barbershop to get a haircut. My barber, Soldier First Class Vertov, has been a legionnaire almost thirty years. He actually fought alongside Cabo Andersen against the wild Berber tribesmen. I have very serious concerns, however, when I realize that he is Russian, and he has very sharp scissors! I also worry that his prying bird-like eyes might detect the big lie concerning my true age.

Almost immediately, he senses that I am German, remarking, "I hate all Fascists!"

To this, I counter in my manliest voice. "I hate all Communists!"

Upon hearing this, he softens a bit, and replies, "So! We agree on one thing, huh? We each hate the Communists!"

"No, Soldier First Class!" I answer. "We agree on both things! My sister died believing that Germanys' leaders were noble men. Even I believed it, until I saw them deserting the city. The cowards! Now I hate them even more than the Reds!"

The old Russian barber now has no doubts as to my loyalties. I rise from his chair ten minutes later with the most pampered head in the entire French Legion!

April 30, 1946, and the celebration of the Day of Camerone has arrived. I am now sixteen years old although Legion records indicate that I am nineteen on this day. I am disappointed because I was not chosen to read about the battle of Camerone.

Headquarters staff members found an actual eighteen-year-old for this reading, and most of us enjoyed hearing it very much. Since I am really younger than the recruit that was selected, then Legion tradition has been broken. Oh, well! "Greta. Is my secret another of your soft truths?"

The Legion band is playing beautiful music. "The March of the Legion" is my favorite. The band also warms the hearts of all Germans by playing familiar marching tunes. The Belgians do not like one song about sausages. "Viva la Legion!"

There are extra rations of wine for the holiday. Many men drink until satisfied. Many men drink until the beasts within them are very close to being unleashed. Fortunately, the NCOs have anticipated that situation, and the flow of wine is abruptly halted.

I decide to take advantage of Blackie's mild stupor to quiz him regarding his oft-repeated remark about women's cooking. When I question him about this, he replies. "Beautiful women should frolic naked in the bedroom, not labor in the kitchen with their aprons and spoons. The time wasted by a saucy woman in the kitchen could be more appreciated in the bedroom. Now let me be! You might wear a uniform, but you are still a boy! When it is time, I will tell you about women!" Blackie foolishly believes that I know nothing of the pleasures of women. I always listen when the older men speak of the women.

*****

Sergent-chef Wimmer begins our bayonet lesson today with an inspirational speech. "Legionnaires, the bayonet is your most import-ant weapon. You will kill with it many times. You and your enemy will face each other, standing on the same small piece of earth. Your enemy will be close enough for you to smell the fear of his breath. Your enemy will be close enough for you to see the death in his eyes.

His last vision…his last image on earth…will be that of you driving your bayonet deep into his mongrel heart. Legionnaires charging forward with bayonets fixed are unstoppable. It is our tradition. Learn your drills well!"

The actual drills involved doing the same maneuvers over and over and over. Thrust! Parry! Thrust! Parry! This is boring, but still, it is my school, and this is my lesson for today. We practice a series of bayonet charges with our rifles loaded—advancing, lunging with bayonets, aiming, firing, reloading, and advancing further. We learn to work as one unit, not as one man. Learning to cooperate is the most valuable lesson of all!

*****

There is news of trouble in the French colonies of Indochina. Rebellious communists have attacked the French. We learn that Legion soldiers are already posted there, and it is rumored that many more may be ordered to go there soon.

Some of the veterans have experienced service in Indochina. They tell us of its deceptive beauty and unforeseen perils. Soldier First Class Vertov, the Russian, is now my good friend and personal barber. He has heard many tales from Indochina. These adventures have been shared with him by the scores of returnees who have sat in his barber chair. They spoke to him of the beautiful city of Saigon in the south. Legionnaire Vertov has heard countless tales of beautiful *congais*. These women are paid to be the temporary wives of the legionnaires stationed there. The young girls are eager to earn money in this way. The few francs the *congais* earn are shared with their parents who consider this arrangement to be both honorable and profitable.

The communist rebels show no mercy in battle. They often execute their wounded prisoners. It is rumored that there are thousands of them in the mountains of the northern Tonkin region. The Viets lie hidden, unseen, until it is too late! They have little need of military skill, since they crush their foe by attacking with surprise. This is a common tactic of the guerillas. The Viets are poorly armed.

Most carry weapons that have been seized from previous battles with the Japanese and French. Their ammunition comes from the stores and depots of the many overrun garrisons in their paths. Opium is plentiful in the highlands, and the rebels use the profits from its sale to buy weapons along the Chinese border. Barber Vertov tells me to prepare for service in Indochina because it will be my destiny. He is a wise man.

******

I am currently learning how to drive a small truck. Driving is fun, but there is great responsibility also. Regular maintenance of the trucks is necessary to ensure that they will be operational when they are needed. Later, I will learn to drive a truck that is large enough to transport an entire squad—and all of the squad's equipment too. This afternoon and tomorrow morning, there will be classes on the use of different types of explosives and land mines. During these lessons, there will be demonstrations of things being blown up. Trucks and exploding bombs are excellent subjects for school! I work hard to be a good student.

CHAPTER 6

Graduation day arrives in the middle of May. We poor souls were herded through those gates just a few months ago, and now we are Legionnaire Soldiers Second Class. My graduating company, comprised of men from various countries, trades, and religions, is now closer to resembling one personality. We now have renewed hope and a purpose in our lives as legionnaires. You might say that we now fit into that mold described to us by the sergent-major on our first day here in Bel Abbes!

We are happy and feeling handsome in our new garrison uniforms of khaki blouses with the green ties. My trousers fit properly, and so do the new black boots. We have been issued our white kepis, which we now wear proudly for our graduation ceremony. After today, the white kepis will be stored away with our gear and worn only for special occasions. Guenther and Blackie seem to be pleased with the new uniforms.

The band stops playing long enough for the commandant himself to deliver a rousing speech. Though his French is lost on many, his message is still clearly understood. "Through your spirit, sacrifice, and loyalty, you are now Legionnaires! Viva la Legion!" The celebration that follows his address does not rival the Day of Camerone, but thankfully, to our delight, this current revelry will not end for several days. Weekend passes are being issued!

We welcome our first payday, knowing that we will soon be free to leave the compound. I am excited as the paymaster counts out 500 francs. These represent my enlistment bonus. There is another 1200 francs, which represents my wages for all days served. And then there is an additional 200 francs as a bonus for achieving the honorable rank of Legionnaire Soldier Second Class. This designation is better known by its more common title—Private! I give the paymaster a snappy salute, turn, and then exit the building. I am now a man of measured financial influence!

The barrack is deserted. Only a few sleeping dogs remain inside. The celebrating legionnaires have rushed to town, with money to pay for two days of revelry. For many, the freedom and modest sum of money will have disappeared before Monday's reveille.

I am invited to accompany my two friends into town. Blackie has arranged for Cabo Fulci to be our guide into town once we have met Guenther. Guenther is waiting when we arrive at his barrack. When Cabo Fulci says that he wishes for us to meet his wife, Guenther eagerly agrees that is a wonderful idea. He does not know that the corporal's wife is a prostitute and that she can be bought for fifty francs. Blackie and I hesitate awkwardly before responding to the old corporal's invitation to meet his wife. Our hesitation provokes a hearty laugh from Cabo Fulci, while Guenther becomes even more confused. Why would his friends react so awkwardly and rudely to a kind invitation from a gracious old legionnaire?

"No! No! It is not that way at all!" a smiling Fulci explains. He is merely inviting us to his house where his wife will be preparing a grand dinner for his homecoming. His wife's business is very profitable at this time, but she chooses to be with him now that he is idle. Now that we fully understand the old corporal's true intentions, we gladly accept his offer of hospitality. Guenther says nothing. He is still confused. Perhaps, I will explain later so that he can share a laugh with us.

After it is settled, the four of us set out together. Fulci is excited, for now he has two full days with his wife, Samira. He will also share his food with his new friends. As we walk, the corporal tells us that his wife will be very happy when she discovers he has brought friends to dine with them. She is Moroccan, from the small town south of Casablanca. They have been married many years. He says that we are in for a wonderful treat because Samira is an excellent cook. When she was very young, her mother taught her the ways of Moroccan, French, and Sudanese cooking.

Corporal Fulci intrigues us further. He tells how slave traders brought Samira's mother to Morocco from the Sudan many years before Samira was born. Later, when Samira was a young girl, her mother was befriended and given food by legionnaires. She became a camp follower, dragging Samira along with her. Every time the Legion camp would move to a new location, the two of them would trail behind, cooking and washing for the soldiers. Fulci explains that was how he met Samira.

Cabo Fulci informs us of customs to be followed in the taking of food in a Muslim home. Although he avows to be a heathen Catholic and declares that Bel Abbes is his Vatican, he has always respected the ways of his wife's family.

As we continue our walk, he explains, "Eat with the fingers of the right hand only. That is simple! We will wash our hands at the table before dining and after dessert. You, Europeans, may not know which dish is dessert because Moroccan food can sometimes be very sweet. Mmmmm, my German friends, good food is meant to be shared!"

As we continue in our walk, the stench of animal dung becomes strong. We meet natives, guiding their donkeys through the streets at midmorning. Two men on the street are shouting loudly at each other. It appears that their arguing will never end. We pass by as they continue. The street is narrow, and we are forced to step aside as a flock of frightened sheep is quickly herded by us. Cabo Fulci warns us to step carefully, lest we dirty our clean boots with sheep dung. We are almost there!

We arrive at the corporal's simple dwelling to be greeted and invited into the front room by Samira. She does not seem surprised by our arrival. I sense that, perhaps, Cabo Fulci has opened his home to friends before on other occasions. Samira seems pleased to have guests in her home, even though our presence fills the largest room. The aromas from many fragrant spices and herbs linger in the air. I look about. There is a colorful but wellworn rug in the front room as well as a glass cabinet with three shelves. The top shelf contains a sacred book, while the other shelves are empty.

Samira's light-brown feet are bare. She wears a dress that is common among the women of this region. Cabo Fulci says that the dress is called a caftan. A dark scarf covers her head but not her interesting face. It is clear to me that she was a very beautiful woman when she was young. She returns to the kitchen, while Fulci encourages us to relax and enjoy our escape from Legion duties.

Wonderful smells from the kitchen continue to fill the air. Cabo Fulci entertains us with his memories of the old Legion. As a young private, he was in charge of the pack mules. This was a great responsibility, he adds. He was stationed in Morocco in 1930, during the fierce Berber uprising, and that was when he met Samira and her family. They share the same year of birth, 1899. The two of them married but were separated for several years during the Big War. He recalls how insane these times were for him, fighting as an Italian beside other Italians and Germans in the French Legion assigned to the British Army in Libya, while fighting against other Italians and Vichy French and, of course, Germans! Upon hearing this, Guenther sits up straight and clears his throat. To pass time until dinner, Fulci offers an English cigarette to the two smokers of our group. It is another fine gesture by the generous corporal.

He tells us that Samira is very quiet and seldom speaks while at home, but when she does talk, it could be in Arabic, French, or Italian. Fulci says that she only speaks German when she is working. Upon hearing this, Blackie, Corporal Fulci, and I enjoy a hearty laugh, while poor confused Guenther can only sit quietly. What can be so funny about that, he must wonder. Fulci adds that Samira knows how to say no in fourteen different languages. Guenther listens silently as the three of us share another outrageous laugh.

We amuse ourselves with a deck of cards, and the time passes quickly. Fulci commends me for being a good trainee. He says that I should make the Legion my permanent home and, someday, become a proud corporal like himself. He mentions Camerone and how, even though it happened in the last century, the day has only been celebrated regularly for fifteen years. He proudly claims that he, barber Vertov, and Cabo Andersen were there together in Algeria for the very first Day of Camerone. This is a remarkable story.

The smells drifting through the small rooms slowly overwhelm us. Several hours have passed, and just when I think that I can take no more, Samira appears in the kitchen doorway and announces that it is time to prepare for dinner. Fulci directs us into a tiny alcove adjacent to the kitchen, where we take our seats on soft plump cushions which have been scattered around a low table. From here, we can smell smoking charcoals and cooked apples.

Our hostess remains standing as the four of us take our seats at the table. Once we are thought to be comfortable, Samira places a cloth towel and a copper bowl filled with water in front of her husband. Corporal Fulci demonstrates by slowly dipping his hands in the water and then drying them with the towel. We do as he has demonstrated.

Next, we are served a single plate, which contains a small baked pastry, or pie, that has been sprinkled with sugar. Fulci is correct! The pie is sweet with cinnamon and very delicious. This dish is already a pleasant memory for my three comrades as they wait patiently for me to finish my own.

"My wife's delicious pigeon pie is the envy of this region!" exaggerates the proud Fulci. "I hope you enjoyed it!"

Samira now brings spoons and forks and a large bowl filled with a stewed mixture. We each take a generous serving in our bowls. As I am still somewhat cautious; I take only a small bite. The stew is seasoned with very hot spices which I am not accustomed to, but I am soon eating it with much enjoyment. I look up momentarily to see that my friends have finished and are, once again, waiting for me to do the same.

Our host informs us that we have just eaten a stew known as tajine. His wife's tajine has been prepared with apples, carrots, artichokes, perhaps, almonds, some roots from the market and, lastly and most important, the remainder of that same poor pigeon that was not included in the earlier pigeon pies.

Cabo Fulci continues. "That was a fat tender pigeon, however! And very fresh too, was it not? Samira tells me that she caught it this very morning. She places her trap on the roof when we have need for a bird."

Samira now places a platter of skewered meat before her husband, and it is passed around the table. I cannot identify the spicy tender meat of the kabobs; however, I sense that it might be lamb. I am certain of only one thing. It is not pigeon! I finish with my kabob just as the good corporal begins to tell us what we have just enjoyed.

"My comrades, were the kabobs tender enough for you? Samira marinates the meat in delicious spices and then braises them slowly over charcoals of just the right temperature until they are perfect. I am a very fortunate fellow!" He laughs. We have just eaten the hump of a camel. I would eat more, but that which remains is for our hostess.

She now presents another large container in front of her husband. This one is covered with a round, cone-shaped lid, which Cabo Fulci removes so that he may admire its contents. He spoons the pasty mush onto his plate, then passes the container. This dish is quickly enjoyed. Samira has returned with a bowl filled with a salad of green leaves and chopped radishes.

Fulci speaks. "My friends, a salad is just a salad, but when it is prepared and served by someone dear to you, then it is a blessing from Allah!" He speaks again, this time while leering playfully at Samira. "Gentlemen, I am confused. I believe that the fine *seksou*, the wonderful dish we have just eaten, contained more of that same poor pigeon!" We laugh as we take salad.

He continues to entertain us. "Allah has blessed this house with either the largest pigeon in all of Algeria or Samira, my dear wife, has deceived me once again by secretly, and foolishly, squandering our pitiful fortune on a skinny chicken from the market!" Fulci is full of humor today.

She now serves each of us a small plate on which there is another pastry. Corporal Fulci tells us that we are now enjoying dessert. This pastry is filled with a paste of creamed almonds. It is a perfect ending, and we know that once again, it is time to wash our hands. Even though I have only used my right hand, I will do like everyone else and wash both.

Samira serves cups of hot sweet tea. There are sprigs of green mint in the tea to give it a special flavor. I enjoy the tea because I have not had anything to drink during the meal.

We each stand and bow respectfully to our quiet hostess as Guenther tells her that we will always remember her for her excellent food and kindness to strangers. Our host invites us to join him in the front room, where Blackie and Guenther are offered another English cigarette. Corporal Fulci uses this time to tell us of his plans. It seems that his retirement and pension will not be forthcoming soon as he had previously hoped. He has chosen to remain a legionnaire for five more years, explaining that the extension was necessary to increase his pension benefits. He now expects to retire in 1951, on a pleasant day in June.

Fulci begins with tales of the Legion. I sense that may be the primary reason the corporal has invited us into his home. He needs someone to entertain with his interesting stories, and it is our good fortune that he has chosen us.

He tells us there was time in Legion history when the white kepi was the only headgear worn. It was common to see Legion road builders and sappers toiling with their picks and shovels in the hot sun. Sweaty cooks could be seen washing pots and kits while up to their elbows in dirty hot water—and all wearing the kepi blanc—even muleskinners! "Imagine today, seeing these same sights! 'It is a mirage,' you would say. 'My eyes are surely deceiving me,' you would say!"

However, during the time the young Fulci was posted in Morocco, some of the officers thought that the white headgear was an inviting target for the Berbers, so they ordered everyone to dye their kepis in black coffee. "We mutinied, however, and refused the order. But the mutiny was really our way of showing disdain for the Berbers' marksmanship." He adds, "We were not fools altogether because we knew full well that in the hot African sun, our brains would cook like eggs in the dark kepis."

Cabo Fulci says the kepi blanc remained as part of the uniform during the Big War and then it was discontinued. He says that today, it is only worn regularly by the Legion band and those involved in special ceremonies.

As darkness nears, the corporal rises to light an oil lantern. It is the proper time for us to express our thanks before leaving to join other celebrating legionnaires. Samira has remained in the kitchen where she has continued to work quietly. She is summoned so that we may each express our enjoyment with the feast she has prepared for us. She is happy that we were pleased. As we leave, I think about our recent feast. Poor Blackie!

This evening, he was compelled to eat food prepared in a kitchen by a woman who truly, truly belongs in the bedroom! Later, for a laugh, I will ask him once again to explain why he dislikes women's cooking.

Cabo Fulci does not accompany us, choosing instead to spend time with his Samira. He cautions us to be vigilant in town because we are sure to encounter black marketers, pickpockets, and beggars. He warns that these culprits spend their entire lives preying on unsuspecting revelers. They move freely and unnoticed around the bazaar district, stalking legionnaires who have celebrated too much. The old corporal woefully adds, "These worms are seldom caught or punished. And their thieving only ends for certain when they die!"

The three of us hurriedly approach a cantina, with a balcony overlooking the street. We quickly enjoy several bottles of beer together and then a bottle of wine. Guenther remarks how similar the red wine is in taste to our very own Legion ration. Blackie laughs and offers that the two wines are, indeed, the same. The wine, which we are now enjoying, has probably been stolen from Legion supplies and then sold for a cheap price to the owner of this business. We agree with Blackie when he says the town's commerce will fail soon if we do not buy another bottle of wine. Guenther says it is our duty to help the merchants, so we buy two bottles!

I sit and talk with Guenther while Blackie seeks the services of a woman in the canteen. He returns an hour later, bragging that the smile on his face was worth the 200 francs he received as a bonus for graduating. We share a big laugh with Guenther after we finally make him aware of Samira's unique secret. We enjoy several more bottles of the cheap Moroccan beer before we stagger back to the compound. Our walk is interrupted once by the sounds of breaking glass and raucous laughter coming from a darkened alley.

CHAPTER 7

Now that we have completed our training, new duties await us. Blackie has been assigned to the Third Regiment of Legion Infantry, or the Third REI, as it is better known as. The regiment is garrisoned throughout French Indochina, having arrived there in June when we were just graduating. Blackie will leave this week by ship to join in the fight against the rebel uprising.

*****

Guenther and I now share permanent quarters in the same barrack. Our legion lives are very different, however. He has been assigned to Headquarters and works in the post print shop, which produces the Legion newspaper. The shop is a very noisy place when the huge printing presses are in operation. Guenther looks fit. He tells me that he has grown much stronger from constantly lifting the heavy galleys of lead type. Guenther says the Heidelberg and Kluge presses were manufactured in Germany, and they are cousins of those formerly used in his own shop in Cologne.

Legionnaire 494321 is presently attending classes at the post hospital on field medicine. The instructors are very direct. They tell us to learn our lessons well because there will be many opportunities to apply our training later. They stress the value of the Legion's tradition of leaving no wounded on the field of battle. Since Legion blood is only being shed in Indochina, there can be little doubt as to our fate.

Presently, we are learning simple treatments. I study hard. Thus far, I have learned to fashion splints as well as functional litters from any materials that might be at hand. The instructors test the makeshift litters to see if they will support the weight of our injured subjects. I can prevent a person from bleeding to death by using four different methods. I am able to recognize and treat the symptoms of shock, sunstroke, and heat exhaustion. I learn the different types of bandages and dressings as well as the particular kinds of wounds or injuries they are suited for. We are schooled on the symptoms and treatment of malaria. Westerners and Europeans living in tropical climates are very vulnerable to this scourge. The treatment for dehydration is also stressed in our instruction. The lesson on dehydration has already been taught and learned well by Legionnaire 494321. It was taught during the days of those grueling marches in the hot desert sun. My training will be completed in few weeks, and then I will most certainly receive a posting elsewhere.

Blackie leaves by rail tomorrow for Casablanca. From there, he will sail to Saigon City. It is with the heaviest of hearts that Guenther and I see him off. Our friendship has been honest now for over a year. I know that he is a good man. He is strong, courageous, and a man I can trust. I am confident that he will eventually find the peace he seeks. Already, he seems happier. Cabo Fulci joins us for the send-off, which is brief. It ends solemnly with a toast of cognac.

"*Bon chance*, Legionnaire Blackie!" snaps Corporal Fulci.

"*Auf Weidersehen*, Private Otto Bak!" responds Guenther with a snappy salute.

I can only add, "Goodbye, Friend."

And then he is gone!

*****

My first-aid training continues on for several weeks. After successfully passing a difficult examination, I qualify to receive additional medical training at a later time. As the days progress, I receive instructions in a variety of other subjects—landmine detection, map reading, compass sighting, and small unit maneuvers. There is training with other weapons—the rifle-grenade, mortar, semiautomatic rifle, and an American rocket tube, which the Amis call a bazooka. This weapon fires a rocket that explodes when it hits its target. It is very different from the rocket launchers we used in the streets of Berlin, but the destructive force is similar.

It has been my fortune to remain in Bel Abbes now for all this time. Life here is presently simple and boring. Guenther is not bored. He is challenged by his job at the printing office. He is always busy setting type or managing the operation of the various letterpresses. His forearms show evidence of the constant lifting of the heavy lead type. This labor of body and mind has been good for Guenther. Perhaps, it has helped to reduce the anguish he feels over the loss of his wife and son. It has been one year since that Christmas in Cologne.

CHAPTER 8

The biggest news arrived today. A general order has been issued directing three hundred legionnaires to ready for transport to Indochina. Those whose numbers are posted will leave Bel Abbes in three days and travel by rail to Casablanca. From there follows a month-long sea voyage of 7,500 miles. My number is there, as well as Guenther's and those of our original cadres—Sergent-Chef Wimmer, and Corporals Andersen and Fulci. The NCOs are more surprised with these orders than we are!

I rush to tell Guenther, only to find that the news has already reached him. The print shop has always had spies at Headquarters. Informants had recently overheard reports from Hanoi concerning attacks on many legion outposts in the Tonkin region. Legionnaires from the Third REI are thought to have manned these garrisons, and it is rumored that many were killed when the Viets overran them. This is news of great significance. The men from Bel Abbes are being assigned to the Third Regiment as replacements for those lost in these disastrous battles.

I am concerned for Blackie's regiment! Guenther says that it will be many months before the names of those who have been killed are compiled. It will be even longer before they are made known to the public. This disastrous news is certain to alarm those with comrades in the Third REI.

It is a busy time…a quickstep time. We are issued additional gear and then we receive a hasty battery of new inoculations. We work feverously packing wooden crates full of stores that will be needed for the journey. On the last day here in Bel Abbes, I say goodbye to barber, Alexander Vertov. We enjoy a toast of schnapps from the bottle in the cabinet behind his barber chair. I will miss the stories of his wonderful adventures, but who can truly say whether I will return to this place someday…maybe to hear more stories and, perhaps, tell a few of my own?

The train ride to Casablanca is comfortable as we have cushioned seats to sit on. We arrive at the largest port city in western Morocco and proceed to board our ship. Several berths of the port are filled with barges loaded with salvage equipment. Workers can be seen swarming over the hulk of a sunken French battleship that sits on the bottom of the harbor. Floating salvage barges and their busy crews work alongside the giant warship.

I am surprised when I discover there is a number painted on the bow of our ship where her name should be—*LS 647*. We learn from the dockworkers that she is a former American freighter that was used during the war to transport captured Germans to prisoner-of-war camps in North America. This is unfortunate news and a very hard truth.

Three companies of African soldiers board the ship with us. They are destined for duty in Indochina as well. There is one light company each from Algeria, Morocco, and Senegal. The chattering Senegalese troops are the blackest men that I have ever seen… and also the tallest…and also the skinniest. These African soldiers are replacements for those already posted in Indochina with French Colonial forces.

Within hours, *LS 647* sails from port with almost 700 men and 90 tons of cargo. We travel due south, with the western coast of Africa slowly disappearing from view. It is very crowded because the ship was not designed to transport this many men. The ship's crew instructs us in lifeboat drills and evacuation measures to follow in the event of fires or other emergencies. I relax to await a great adventure.

*****

The days at sea are dull and routine. There is a schedule that must be followed in order to allow everyone equal time on the decks for exercise, drills, and fresh air. Conditions below deck, in the crowded holds where we live and sleep, are challenging. Our current ordeal aboard *LS 647* must be remarkably similar to that of my countrymen who were transported by her years earlier during the war. There is very little water available for body hygiene as it must be saved for drinking. The breathable air is caustic and fouled with bodily stench, but for once, no one blames this on Cabo Andersen.

Many men are pale, being overcome with a seasickness made worse by a diet of greasy canned rations. The sick ones are cursed regularly by the healthy for contributing even more to the unpleasantness of this voyage. This time at sea, languishing in these conditions, is a greater challenge than even that of the dreaded daily route marches. Some are convinced they would be better off jumping over the side into the water. Cabo Andersen says that these men are merely experiencing *le cafard*, a type of mental suffering that is unique to tormented legionnaires everywhere.

*****

I do not know how the Africans are faring since we are separated from their part of the ship at all times. For reasons unknown to us, we have been ordered not to communicate or fraternize with these soldiers. One evening, however, I found myself to be cornered on all sides unexpectedly by three smiling drunken soldiers from one of these companies. I did not recognize their nationality, but I can only say they were "neither black nor thin or skinny!" I quickly realized that my situation was desperate when two of them suddenly pinned me tightly between the cargo containers, while the third man began to stroke my arms and shoulders. I struggled to resist, but my efforts were useless against their strength of numbers!

It was my very good fortune that Guenther should appear at this time. Alarmed by the hopelessness of my sorry predicament, he briskly approached my assailants and, with neither hesitancy nor forewarning, smashed his fist into the surprised face of the nearest scoundrel. The powerful force of this lone blow rendered the besotted pig unconscious. He toppled over, falling backward. At this time, the two cursed devils that had been holding me motionless quickly released their grips to better defend themselves from my enraged comrade. It was too late, however, as the intoxicated vermin proved to be no match for Guenther's tremendous strength. He threw one to the ground as easily as one might toss aside an empty overcoat and smiling as he did so! I pounced upon the third and struck him repeatedly with all my might. The two beaten dogs tugged desperately at the clothes of their unconscious colleague, frantically dragging his useless carcass from the deck.

Guenther, pleased with the havoc he had just inflicted upon the trio, boasted proudly. "We marked their faces up good, did we not?" Then he asked, "Dieter, why did you not shout for help? There are many people lingering about who would certainly have heard you? Did they cover your mouth to prevent you from calling out? Those sons of swine would have had their way with you had I not come along just now! You are very fortunate that I did!" He waited for me to speak.

I thought for a moment, then answered. "I have never asked for help from anyone. Any pain or suffering that I must endure will be pain or suffering that I deserved because I was not alert enough to foresee it or strong enough to prevent it!" I paused. "It is a pitiful being who must cry out for help from others to prevent harm from befalling him. I ask you, is this something you would do? Is this something any legionnaire would do? I think not!"

Guenther, surprised by my remarks, hesitated and then replied, "I have just heard the words of a very wise 'fool.' Yes…a wise, proud fool who would rather live the rest of his life tormented by the unpleasant memories of the day his body was violated by pestilent scum because he had wisely concluded in his short wisdom-filled life that the weaklings and unfortunates of the world neither needed help nor deserved it… Ah! What great wisdom this is indeed!"

This unexpected outpouring of personal ridicule stunned me greatly, yet still he was not finished. I waited as he continued. "Would you help me if I cried out for help, or would you consider me to be just another undeserving weakling? Or perhaps Fulci or Blackie… what of them? And what of God? Am I considered weak because I ask Him every day to help me by giving me the strength to continue on without my wife and son? Your logic is that of a selfish person who would deprive man of one of his basic needs—the need to help others." Guenther smiled. "I know you well, Dieter, and you are not a selfish person!"

Guenther had given me much to think about that regrettable evening. I thanked him for rescuing a "wise fool" from the dangers of foolish wisdom. And lastly, I also thanked him factually for "the rescuing of my ass." I remember him remarking that the ordeals of Indochina would likely provide a long overdue justice for many cruel and heartless men of this world—and just possibly including my would-be assailants.

*****

Today, the morning sea is very calm. Last night, however, a rainstorm with raging winds tossed our ship about quite roughly. Each of us feared a watery death. Many became ill in the turbulent storm.

We have sailed across the equator, around the southernmost part of Africa, and are presently traveling in a northeast direction. Daily exercises continue on deck. During this time, we occasionally spy lone steamer ships, always at great distances from our own ship. As the voyage continues, so does our daily ration of wine. The supply of fresh fruit was exhausted after ten days at sea; however, we still receive handfuls of dried dates and nuts. The cooks are complimented for keeping us supplied with black coffee at all hours, but the army bread is gone and has been replaced with tins of hard tasteless biscuits. These are not so bad if one spreads them with the fruit jams and jellies. Wonderful memories of the delicious soupe in Bel Abbes begin to stir me. The tins of field rations are a disappointment. They seem suited best for those nearest starvation. Legion food has spoiled me. Someone who was once so hungry that he envied the food of Russian guard dogs now criticizes the quality of canned army rations.

The freighter's crewmembers often engage us in conversation and supply us with information regarding our changing location and direction. A seaman tells Cabo Fulci and Guenther that we will cross the equator again, this time from south to north. He adds that we are now approaching the narrow straits between Sumatra and Java and land will become visible for the first time in almost one month. The open sea has been very boring, so we eagerly await sight of land.

We approach the Netherlands Indies, and everyone attempts to come onto the crowded deck to witness the passage through the straits. Several fights erupt as men position themselves to get better views of the changing scenery. Loud cursing is overheard in many different languages as the lengthy voyage has challenged the tolerance of most everyone. As the large islands of the strait disappear, they are replaced by the sightings of numerous tiny islands. A crewmember informs me that fierce headhunters and cannibals inhabit many of these same unexplored islands. You do not want to be stranded there.

Our shipmate says that we are now less than one week away from docking in Saigon, where showers of fresh water and hot food await us. Flared tempers subside as the good news travels quickly throughout the ship. Spirits soar, even for those known to be suffering painfully from the lingering effects of dysentery and poisoned stomachs.

CHAPTER 9

At last, we can see the mainland—the mysterious Orient and its many hidden unseen perils. *LS 647* nears Cap Saint Jacques and the entrance to the muddy gray Dong Nai River. The excitement returns again as everyone spill onto the decks for their first view of our new destination. The river is wide at this point and surrounded by flat marshes on both sides that continue unchanged in every direction as far as the eye can see. This view is broken only by the rise of three prominent hills on the nearest shore. The grayish reeds of marsh grass are bent and wavering constantly in the strong coastal breeze.

Cabo Andersen is the first to recognize the rusting wreck of a large Japanese ship destroyed during the war. The sunken vessel appears to have been caught out in the open marsh, with no concealment, and then attacked violently and repeatedly. *LS 647* churns slowly by the ill-fated ship. This unfortunate casualty of the war is not alone, however, as we soon approach two additional sunken vessels of unknown nationalities. Both were useful commerce ships at one time, but now they are nothing more than unsalvageable hulks of rusting steel.

A crewman on deck tells us that the ship's captain has timed his arrival this morning to coincide with the river's highest tide. He says that within hours, we will reach a tributary of the Saigon River, and we will follow it for another hour before docking.

As we continue inland, the riverbanks slowly become stretches of green jungle forests. I am excited to see many monkeys playing and swinging among the different varieties of trees. Colorful flower blossoms of tremendous size surround these trees. We get our first look at the native Easterner as we pass a settlement whose site appears to have been carefully carved from the jungle. Some of the rectangular shaped dwellings, or shelters, sit on stilts high over the muddy river's edge. These inhabitants, or primitives, show little interest in our presence, while we, being deprived of all diversions for thirty-two days, gawk in disbelief.

The many villages of fishermen and boats have become so numerous now that they seem to be connected as one. This must mean that Saigon is near. We continue for a short time, and then legionnaires standing high atop the cargo containers let out a chorus of tremendous yells. They have spied Saigon! The great city remains hidden from our view, however, behind the tight clusters of floating riverfront shacks.

Soon our ship docks at a busy riverfront wharf. Our month-long voyage is now complete. Cranes are busy lifting loads of timber and other cargo from the concrete wharf onto waiting freighters. A brick warehouse of enormous size demands our attention.

Laborers, the first Vietnamese people to be observed up close, are busily involved in various tasks. Dozens of the tiny brown-skinned men are applying a fresh coat of paint to the hull of a large freighter. By using brushes and paint rollers that have been attached to long bamboo poles, each painter's reach is extended considerably. The Viets are suspended high over the water like nervous spiders on rickety planks of scaffolding. These scaffolds hang precariously from ropes thrown over the sides of the freighter. The ship becomes lighter and gradually rises higher in the water as its heavy cargo is being unloaded. This exposes even more of the ship's unpainted surface. Although at first appearing to be comical as well as dangerous, the Viet's method of ship painting now seems to be very practical.

We disembark with our gear in an orderly fashion at the direction of the NCOs. We attempt a brisk march from the wharf to the nearby military district, but our legs do not cooperate. They have been at sea for too long. We also discover that the midday humidity and heat combine to set upon each of us in a most oppressive fashion. Nonetheless, we doggedly drag ourselves into the French military compound where we receive assignments to barracks. These barracks are graciously equipped with water for showers and washing. Orders are immediately posted, granting everyone three days of light duty.

Examinations are being scheduled at the large army hospital for those needing long-awaited medical treatments. Our first night in Saigon is filled with restful sleep, even though the distant thundering sounds of artillery outside the city continue all night.

Guenther and I remain hopeful that our friend Blackie is alive and safe.

Three days pass quickly. The limited activity had been deemed necessary to hasten our recovery from the physical and mental adversities of the voyage as well as recovery from another battery of unexpected inoculations. Several men have deserted, but the typhoid and typhus shots were not to blame. As in fact, every one of the yellow-tails waited until after he had been properly immunized before disappearing into the crowded city. The scoundrels knew they would be doomed rats in the disease-ridden climate of the tropics. And though they are still rats, they are now protected from malaria, cholera, tetanus, smallpox, typhoid fever, and typhus.

Our barracks are comfortable, but the windows must remain open at all times to cool the air. This is an invitation to the dozens of lizards that lurk about outside. These slinky creatures like to come inside to feast on the large numbers of bugs and insects. The lizards are nervous of us and are easily frightened away. The water and sweet soap refresh our uniforms and bodies. The food has been generally acceptable here in the compound, but many complain that the breakfast lacks substance. Coffee is served with bread, cheese, and fruit jelly. The cooks inform us that we are eating the regular French army breakfast, and if we do not like it, then it is too bad because that is all we will be served.

Everyone is active, taking advantage of the precious gift of time to prepare. Cabo Fulci longs for Samira. He writes her a letter in which he expresses confidence in her faithfulness of heart. Although there is plenty of water, I witness Cabo Andersen busy washing his feet and uniform in the same bucket of soapy water. When I question him about this extremely conservative use of water, he snaps back.

"If you had been deprived of water for three days by bandits in the Syrian Desert, then you too might see things as I do! It is sinful to use good water for anything other than drinking. Is that so difficult for you to understand, Chapeau?" So that is why this old veteran of many desert campaigns has chosen to refrain from bathing altogether?

The French soldiers in the garrison have recommended that we visit an establishment known as Buffalo Park. Cabo Fulci says that this is the largest brothel in all of Asia, and a place to avoid at all costs. Nonetheless, many from our group, including Sgt. Wimmer, are there now. Fulci, Guenther, and I decide to explore this strange new city on our own. We walk to a large cathedral, passing many businesses on the broad tree-lined boulevard.

The Vietnamese are active people. There are some automobiles and military trucks on the largest street. Many people, most of them being Westerners, prefer to be transported by a strange vehicle that is nothing more than a double seat fastened to the front of a tricycle. Vietnamese males power these cycles known as cyclos-pousses, or pedi-cabs.

Young women and schoolgirls are seen wearing long white shirts with black skirts or black pants. I am quickly alerted to their gentle beauty. How swiftly they move about. Merchants are standing everywhere, selling jewelry, colorful fabrics, flowers, and men's haircuts. Restaurants and outdoor cafes have many happy customers. Occasionally, we pass buildings, and I am reminded of home and Germany. There are small parks with large trees to shade us from the burning sun. The streets off the main boulevard are not as pleasant. Adults and small children are seen sleeping soundly on the warm sidewalks. On most corners, men can be seen throwing paper money onto the street as they gamble at different games of chance. We find these buildings are nothing more than shacks separated by narrow alleys. These alleys are occupied by vendors with displays of merchandise, raw food, cooked food, and crates of very smelly fish. There are equal numbers of dogs and beggars.

Upon returning to the compound, Cabo Andersen tells us that the police have apprehended two of the deserters. They were arrested when a merchant identified them as being the same men who had beaten and robbed him two days earlier. It is very unlikely that we will ever see these men again.

CHAPTER 10

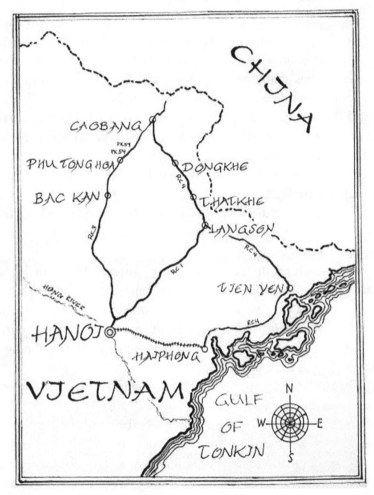

Map by J. S. Reese

A week in Saigon has passed, and we are now being ordered
to Hanoi in the uppermost Tonkin region of Indochina. This news

comes with little surprise because we know the communist Viet Minh are most active in this area. *LS 647* has been hastily made ready for this voyage north. The Senegalese and North Africans will not be traveling with us as they have already been diverted to posts elsewhere. For the two-day journey to the port of Haiphong, we will share our transport with a unit of French army sappers and their roadbuilding equipment, which has already been loaded.

We reach Haiphong by sailing up the coast and then up a wide river to the mainland, docking at one of the many large concrete berths. As we march to the train station, I can see that Haiphong, like Saigon, has many modern buildings, built of solid brick and stone, and broad tree-lined streets. Our stay here is brief. We go by rail to Hanoi, while the French engineers and their machines travel by a highway, known as Route Colonial 4, to the same destination. We enter the city after crossing over the Red River on the Doumer Bridge. The large well-used bridge has been designed for both rail and highway traffic.

Tall African soldiers armed with machine guns guard the long bridge on both sides. I believe the smiling black men may be from Senegal.

After reaching the enormous brick railroad station in Hanoi, we are then crowded onto the backs of trucks and driven to a busy military installation. We are told not to unpack our trunks because we will be leaving again very early in the morning. I stagger onto a bed and fall asleep thinking of tomorrow and the pretty schoolgirls in Saigon. I will soon be seventeen.

The next day, Guenther, Corporal Andersen, Sergent Wimmer, myself, and thirty men from our original group are issued rifles, ammunition, and canteens for water. We board trucks and travel north on Route Colonial 3, or more commonly, RC 3, to a small village called Phu Tong Hoa. We join a company of legionnaires that has been stationed here for over a year. The commanding officer, a captain, and the senior NCO, a sergent, anxiously greet our arrival. They are greatly relieved to find that our journey from Hanoi has been without incident. Quarters have already been arranged for us in an old stone building. This building also serves as a warehouse for the company. The part of the encampment where we have been assigned to live is surrounded completely by a continuous hedge of sharpened bamboo stakes. These are planted firmly in the ground, with their pointed tips facing outward. A few strands of barbed wire are also visible outside the primitive defense of bamboo. Four tall observation towers, constructed of larger bamboo, are strategically placed just inside the barriers of sharp stakes and wire.

Two vigilant sentries occupy each tower. Nearby, high mountains of thick jungle trees enclose the village of Phu Tong Hoa on all sides. Dark motionless clouds fill a gray sunless sky.

Private Lindler, a Pole, chooses to befriend us while our NCOs receive a special briefing by the captain and his lieutenant, the only Frenchman in the garrison. Legionnaire Lindler has been here for a full year. He is eager to hear about our recent travels and any news from the other world, just as we are anxious to learn more about life here.

He tells us that the Viet Minh rebels are dangerous and grow stronger every day. They have threatened to destroy the village and kill everyone here but, thus far, have only succeeded with attacks on the smaller undefended villages in the surrounding countryside. They are ruthless! They collect taxes and take large supplies of rice from the peasants without payment. They systematically assassinate those who deal with the French colonialists. Lindler says that many of the villagers have been forced to watch these murders. Frequently, the Viet Minh shoot at convoys on RC 3, both north and south of the village. They also mine the highway under cover of darkness and cause much damage and many casualties. Observation airplanes are useless when trying to detect the rebels because they have the jungle to hide in. And when they do choose to leave the cover of the jungle, they remain invisible because they are so skillful at concealing their presence. They maintain their individual camouflage from freshly cut foliage, and when they are moving through the countryside, they are known to change the foliage frequently to match the terrain around them as it also changes. They are very determined to drive us away.

Private Lindler continues, saying that the communists have spies and paid informants in Phu Tong Hoa. These spies inform the

Viets in advance of all the company's movements. Opportunities to snare the guerillas in their jungle nests are very rare because of this situation. Yet, surprise is the Viets' greatest weapon.

They employ tricks to inflict as many casualties as possible and to weaken our resolve to remain here. Deep pits are dug in the ground and then set firmly with sharpened stakes—or deadly, poisonous vipers. My eyes widen at this mention of poisonous snakes. Smaller punji pits are designed to both trap and maim those who are so unfortunate as to step into one of them. "And many do!" he adds without hesitation.

He continues by telling how the guerillas stretch tiny, undetectable wires across trails throughout the countryside. These wires are attached to grenades or other crude inventions that explode when touched. Many have died this way. Guenther and I listen carefully to every word from the mouth of the experienced stranger. After all, his wiles and good fortune have allowed him to survive thus far. He says that the guerillas are now armed with heavy mortars and have used them effectively against another outpost near Bac Kan. He considers the Viets' possession of heavy mortars to be a very disturbing matter but adds that we will prevail because the Legion's spirit is not easily crushed.

Legionnaire Lindler is happy that we are here to add to the garrison's strength of only eighty men. At least one legionnaire has either been killed or wounded every week for several consecutive months, and we are the first replacements for those that have been lost.

He admits that he has presented a very disturbing view of our situation but not to worry because the veterans here have learned to adapt to this cunning foe with tricks of our own. Besides, we have better weapons and use them with greater skill. "Life here can be pleasant," he encourages, mentioning the good food and abundant supply of alcohol. Several of his comrades have acquired *congayes* as mistresses, while captured rebels become laborers and do much of the physical work around the encampment. He knows of no one called Blackie, or Private Bak, but suggests that we talk with some of the other German legionnaires who may have had a chance meeting with our friend.

Lieutenant Sens, a graduate of the French military academy, Saint-Cyr, is the only officer here other than Captain Castel, the CO. Sergent Wimmer and Corporal Andersen are replacing two NCOs who were killed two months before when their carrier hit a road mine and plunged into a deep ravine. Wimmer and Andersen, along with Sergent Latallo and five other corporals, are the only sous-officers for the entire company. Four men of Asian stock serve as scouts and interpreters. They live here with the garrison also. Three are darker-skinned Tai tribesmen from one of the numerous remote mountain villages further north. They are quiet and smile most of the time. The three are known as Red Tais because the women of their tribe wear red clothing. The other native scout's origin is unknown. His name is Vu, and he makes every effort to please me for reasons that I do not understand. When he is not on an assignment, he follows me everywhere I go, happily smiling all the time. Vu is certainly not an interpreter as he can offer only a few words of French, and these, only with much effort. My few attempts to communicate with him thus far have failed. Most of the legionnaires are German, but there are also Bulgarians, Belgians, Russians, Poles, Slavs, Spaniards, and Italians in the company. There is even an Englander posted here. He is pleasant and, as with the Russians, an undeclared peace exists between us.

*****

Convoys from Hanoi must bring needed supplies every week, but they never follow the same schedule as this would certainly welcome trouble. It is our duty to patrol RC 3 north of Phu Tong Hoa to the fortified blockhouse at Poste Kilometrique 54. This is a very dangerous assignment because we must look for recently hidden land mines, while the unseen Viets wait for the perfect moment to attack us. Road-sweeping patrols frequently come under fire from the steep mountain cliffs which dominate most of the road from Phu Tong Hoa beyond PK 54. This geography offers great opportunities for the skittish Viets, who prefer to disappear quickly after they have sprung their traps. We ride in armored carriers, but they are vulnerable to the very same road mines that we are dispatched to look for. Today, we searched five kilometers of highway in two hours and found nothing. However, as we return to the village, none of us can be certain that the guerillas are not presently laying mines in areas that we have just swept.

*****

We regularly patrol the surrounding countryside on foot. This is reassuring to those villages that still remain deeply suspicious of the guerillas and their cause. Our patrols always leave the security of the encampment under cover of darkness and the treacherous eyes of those who might warn the Viets. Each member of the patrol is expected to satisfactorily manage the weight of weapons, food, canteens of water, and munitions. Our packs seem even heavier as the day becomes unbearably hot. I think that even a healthy, strong mule would be robbed of his will in these conditions. The canteen water is cool and refreshing in the early morning, but by noonday, it must be cautiously taken because it has become hot enough to burn one's lips. Our uniforms are soaked with perspiration, and salt tablets must be taken to prevent a painful cramping of limbs. These tablets create discomfort in the stomach, but a worse penalty is experienced if they are not taken. When the cramps overtake a soldier, the entire patrol must halt until he recovers well enough to continue. Some operations have failed simply because there was not enough water for those involved.

*****

The monsoon rains have begun. This first rain is a signal to the rice farmers, telling them that it is time to begin planting their seedlings. The water buffaloes struggle mightily to pull their wooden harrows through the stubborn wet muck of the paddy fields. The workers do not look up when we walk by but continue as if we are invisible. The violent downpours are a welcomed relief from the infernal heat, but these cool respites are usually temporary. When the clouds finally lift away, an even more-vengeful sun returns to steam your wits. Fields of elephant grass grow everywhere. This saw-bladed grass stands taller than any of the men, who are sometimes obligated to walk through it. One must be aware of wild raspberry bushes. Their needle-sharp thorns can rip your flesh as well as your uniform.

The terrain is difficult to move through. If there are no established tracks, we follow dry creek beds or cut our own paths through the tangles of vines and underbrush. The streambeds are now beginning to fill with water from rains higher up in the mountains. The patrol is constantly on the alert for signs of danger. I know to take every step with extreme caution. When we are forced to walk on an established trail, the first man of the patrol always holds a long slender reed, extended well in front of him. If the reed bends slightly for no apparent reason, then this usually indicates the presence of a tripwire which may be connected to a bomb.

I have learned much about the jungle. Its sweet earthy smell comes from its abundance of decaying plants and matter. Rocks, stones, and boulders are especially slippery in the damp jungle forest. This is true even during the driest season.

Care must be taken to remove the tiny green leeches that latch onto our bodies as we pass through the leafy underbrush. The larger blood-sucking brown leeches live in the water and become attached to our legs as we wade the streams. These are easier to detect but harder and more painful to remove. The birds of the jungle are noisy, chirping and flittering about in the treetops. Their silence, however, alerts us to the possibility of an ambush.

My inexperience was never more evident than the day when I foolishly stepped off the trail to relieve myself and tumbled into a waist-deep punji pit. Fortunately for me, this particular trap had been abandoned many years ago, and the sharpened bamboo stakes in the bottom of the pit were rotten. They collapsed under the weight of my body, and I received only a terrible scare and a few scratches.

The nearby villages of bamboo and thatch are almost identical in appearance. They are always constructed in open sunny clearings near the rice fields and vegetable gardens of sweet potatoes, maize, cabbages, peppers, and beans. An underground tuber, called manioc, is also very popular with the villagers. Dogs, pigs, and chickens roam unattended through the village and are often seen sleeping in the cool shade underneath the stilted dwellings. Fish are trapped in some of the paddies and ponds that contain water all year. The fish are layered in a split-bamboo rack and then covered with palm oil. They are then allowed to rot for weeks. The liquid from this decomposing combination is collected in a tray underneath the rack, and then stored in earthen pots. This rotten foul-smelling sauce is called *nuoc-mam*, and it is used by the Vietnamese to add flavor to their otherwise tasteless rice.

The older men and women constantly chew on something called the betel nut, which tends to make their lips red and their teeth unusually black. The villagers supply our cooks with plenty of chickens and fresh eggs, however; but the legionnaires refuse to eat the vegetables grown in their thriving gardens. It seems that the village gardeners enrich their garden soil with the willful addition of human feces.

CHAPTER 11

News reaches us of recent successful attacks by the Viets on some lightly defended outposts north of Phu Tong Hoa. We strengthen our defenses by adding more sandbags to protect the only two light machine guns in the entire company. The NCOs have instructed us to lay hundreds of additional land mines outside the perimeter in areas where they will be helpful if the Viets choose to attack. Weapons are cleaned, and extra ammunition is issued to every man in the company. Wooden crates containing grenades are pried open and distributed to each of the camp's four-corner bastions. We are called to alert when one of the montagnard scouts returns to tell the captain that many, very large groups of well-armed rebels were seen moving toward Phu Tong Hoa. They will be here soon. The sudden news is not received well because this very night will be moonless—a condition that is most favorable to the enemy!

The officers divide us equally into four platoons of fifteen men each. Each platoon is then assigned two NCOs and positioned at one of the four-corner strongholds. For the looming danger, it is my good fortune to be grouped with Guenther, Sergent Wimmer, and another veteran corporal. Vu, my smiling shadow, is also posted with us, but I do not see Cabo Andersen anywhere. We are greatly encouraged when we learn that our position has one of the two lone machine guns in the entire company. Sergent Wimmer inspects our gear. He is confident that our training has prepared us for that which awaits us. Guenther, unlike myself, does not seem excited by the prospect of battle. An unexplainable dread had followed me along the streets and canals of Berlin at the very end, and now, on perhaps the eve of battle, that same feeling is trying to return. I am greatly restored by my training and the words of our leaders. "Follow orders! Do your duty!" Perhaps, that is all we legionnaires need to do to prevail?

As darkness falls, the sentries descend from the watchtowers and take positions with us on the four corners. At exactly 2100 hours, two events happen simultaneously. Mortar shells begin falling at a rate of four per minute, but not one of the rounds explodes within the fortifications. Several trumpets sound loudly in the jungle—a signal to the men hidden there to begin their advance. Hundreds of men suddenly appear, advancing from the forest's edge, yelling wildly, coming straight at us through the darkness. In short time, several of the attacking men fall dead or wounded after running directly into our minefields. They continue advancing across the open terrain now from two directions. More rebels continue to emerge from the jungle to join the attack. When it is apparent that we can wait no longer, the NCOs give us the order to begin firing. Even then, the two machine guns remain silent, waiting until the Viets are closer so they will be more effective. We aim and fire directly into the masses of Viets that are now attempting to blast passages under the hedge of bamboo and barbed wire. This is being attempted by using bags of explosives attached to the ends of long bamboo poles. They are not deterred in the least bit by the accuracy of our rifle fire and continue on with their attempts to blast through our wire. Loud earth-shaking mortar rounds are now beginning to fall within the compound. The red-hot shell splinters hum as they fly dangerously through the air just over our heads.

A gap has finally been opened at one corner, and hundreds of attackers frantically pour through it into the main camp. The legionnaires there pull back to other corners and join in the defense of these positions. A larger breech is now created, and even more of the rebels charge through it. Finally, the machine guns begin rattling. Their deadly fire takes its toll of the enemy and, momentarily, halts their advances. The thick smoke of battle hovers close to the ground, adding to the confusion of both sides. The Viets hesitate, regrouping from their wild, maddening charge through the camp. With this opportunity, we begin to hurl countless grenades into their numbers. They are greatly stunted in their advance by this action. Both machine guns continue chattering with their business of impersonal slaughter. Cries of agony and distress fill the night.

My position holds as others from the fallen corners scurry in for refuge. We supply them with grenades, and they rejoin the battle with us. A breathless soldier crawls into our position and informs us that both officers have been killed. A mortar fatally wounded the lieutenant during the first hour of the attack, while the captain was killed instantly by the blast from an exploding bag of dynamite. The NCOs will have to take over the command's defense. This is sobering news. The Viets are no longer using their mortars since their troops are inside the outpost. This is considered to be to our advantage. The bitter fighting continues on for hours, and I begin to worry when I do not hear the familiar steady sound of the second machine gun. Sergeant Wimmer is concerned as well, since losing the third corner would be catastrophic. At this point, Sergeant Wimmer determines that there are enough legionnaires in this single bastion to mount a counterattack to regain the other machine gun position. He orders everyone who has taken refuge here from the other positions to "attach bayonets." Several of those in my care are seriously wounded and cannot stand, but approximately three-dozen men are able to comply with the order. Behind Sergeant Wimmer, these men advance in short rushes toward the second machine gun position on the west corner. On command from the sergent, they kneel and pour well-aimed fire into the surprised Viets. The wounded legionnaires in our corner who are able to handle their rifles now fire in support of this surprising counterattack.

They swiftly charge through the smoke of battle to reach the corner bastion. Here, they find a dozen otherwise healthy men who readily join them in the attempt to retake the remaining bastions. The machine gun has been silenced by the Viets, but this does not slow the counterattacking legionnaires. Many hurl grenades as they advance, while the main line continues to drop and rain accurate fire into the startled Vietminh hordes. The wounded men are not entirely dispirited as they believe that there is still much fight left in the garrison. After all, many here are not strangers to war.

Meanwhile, the advancing legionnaires have retaken all but the first bastion abandoned to the Viets at the beginning of the battle. Here, the communist rebels face a surprise as the determined shouting legionnaires suddenly emerge through the thick clouds of smoke and are quickly upon them with their bayonets. As daylight arrives, the trumpets in the jungle sound recall—and defeat for two Vietminh regiments.

We, who have survived through the night, are slowly overwhelmed by, of all things, the queer, unnerving quietness resulting from the sudden, unexpected end of the engagement. This eerie pall of silence soon falls away as the carnage of battle becomes more evident. Our rattled senses, which have been jolted unmercifully for six continuous hours, are instantly subdued by the sight of the shocking aftermath. The dead and wounded are sprawled everywhere—in every direction.

We have lost our officers, two NCOs, and twenty-one legionnaires. Unfortunately, these numbers include Private Lindler from Poland. Eighteen comrades have been wounded, while we are unable to determine the Viets' actual losses. They have removed many of their dead and wounded from the field to conceal their true losses. The bodies of those killed in the minefields remain as they fell. The severely injured Viets are being moved to the sugarcane mill at the edge of the village. Here, they will wait to receive attention to their wounds. All the able prisoners, including those already in captivity before the battle, will be used to dig graves for their fallen comrades. This will be done immediately. Our attention to the wounded legionnaires continues.

NCOs Latallo, Wimmer, and Cabo Andersen suddenly appear. I am relieved to know that they are unharmed, just as Corporal Andersen is relieved to know that Guenther and I are safe. Sergent Latallo tells everyone that an armored relief column with medical personnel has been dispatched from Bac Kan, but their progress will be slow because the highway has not yet been cleared of mines. He is very upset with the loss of the captain and young lieutenant

Out of respect for the fallen officers and men, Cabo Andersen suggests that a color guard be formed by the remaining six NCOs to present their bodies to the relief column when it arrives. Sergent Latallo thinks that this is a befitting honor and gives the order. When the relief column finally arrives, they find, to their astonishment, all six noncommissioned officers proudly standing at attention in their white kepis and ceremonial dress uniforms. Sergent Latallo wears a magnificent saber, but even this is not as impressive as the decorated breast of Cabo Andersen. I am certain that the old corporal will tip over if another medal is ever pinned to his impeccable uniform. As the members of the relief column survey the results of the vicious fighting in disbelief, the honor guard, before a formation of forty smoky-eyed survivors, presents arms to our fallen comrades. The officers' bodies are then placed in the back of one of the column's trucks and covered with a canvas sheet which has our regimental flag stitched into its center. The officers will be returned to their families in France, or they may be buried in the military cemetery near Hanoi. The expanding graveyard outside our camp will be the final resting place for the twenty-three legionnaires, who, in the words of Sergent Latallo, "shed their blood for France, but died for *the* Legion!" A soft truth...perhaps? Sergent Wimmer, by his decisive actions today, has made me proud to be a legionnaire, and once again, a German!

*****

The daily struggle to communicate with Vu continues. He is smiling broadly as he points to me. He speaks. It is his customary offering of singsong verse which I now translate from pigeon French to mean "You same children! Children same you!" It seems that this is all he wishes for me to understand, and being content with that, he stubbornly refuses to learn only that which is necessary to keep earning the French money. Vu's message clearly means that he considers me to be an undeveloped man with the nature of a child.

I have learned from the other Laotian scouts that Vu is from a small clan of the Meo tribes—the Lolos. Their remote villages are hidden above the clouds in the very highest mountains of Laos and China. Vu is considered to be the best scout. Except for me, he stays alone, having nothing to do with the Tai interpreters or villagers. He frowns to show his dislike for their fish, *nuoc-mam*, and betel nuts—and yet, he once ate a raw frog in my presence.

CHAPTER 12

Five of us report for duty at the fortified blockhouse on the highway north of PK 54. This isolated one-room fortification of thick concrete walls and blast-proof doors was constructed beside a river to protect a key bridge from Viet saboteurs. We are replacements for five very cheerful legionnaires who have been here for six months. The men are obviously happy to be returning to a less complicated life at Phu Tong Hoa.

The blockhouse leader, a dispirited sergeant, and three other machine gunners, let us know immediately that there is nothing pleasant about this place. We are truly isolated here, with the radio as our only contact to the outside if we need help. Sergeant Cybulski tell us that soupe is limited to army rations, coffee, and fresh fish, which are easily caught by stunning them first with grenades thrown into the river. The wine ration is rigidly controlled by the Polish sergeant to prevent anyone from becoming too unfit for duty. Everyone, except the rooftop lookouts and bridge inspectors, sleeps during the day, since the guerillas are most likely to attack under the cover of darkness. The routine is altered during those days when it is necessary to survey the area around us. These five-man patrols are dispatched in the early mornings when the thick wet fog, or *crachin*, hangs like a blanket in the mountains' lower valleys. Often, this shroud of fine drizzle is so heavy that one can see no more than a few meters in any direction. However, there is no advantage to be enjoyed by the Viets because they cannot see through it either.

The concrete fort, or *la tombe*, as the more experienced veterans call it, appears to be of sturdy construction. A small gasoline-powered generator provides enough electricity to dimly light the inside of the dampened bunker during the day. The lights are turned off at night so that our eyes can adapt more readily to the darkness around us. The light streaming through the narrow firing slits in the black of night would also provide excellent targets for the Viets who constantly watch from the jungle. There are three light machine guns and one Browning automatic rifle inside the dank mold-stained central room, each gun facing outward in a different direction. Sentries reach the outside roof from inside the big chamber by climbing a ladder through the overhead trap door. During an attack, grenades can be thrown great distances from here in any direction. Outside, behind heavy protective walls, there is a sandbagged pit for the lone mortar. The mortar is used primarily to fire illumination flares at intervals throughout the night. The bright, glowing flares sway back and forth under their parachutes as they slowly fall back to earth. These swaying lights create many shadowy images which creep eerily over the cleared land around the blockhouse. It is easy to imagine that all of this movement is somehow threatening when it is night in the jungle.

Sharpened bamboo hedges, identical to those at Phu Tong Hoa, completely encircle the structure. Beyond these, thick coils of rusting barbed wire are tangled high to create an additional barrier. Hundreds of crudely fashioned warning devices hang loosely from the barbed wire. These noisemakers are nothing more than empty ration cans containing a few spent cartridges. The recognizable sound is often heard whenever the blockhouse crew's pet mongoose ventures into the wire to kill another unsuspecting snake. An outer ring of land mine extends further out and up from the river, completely encircling the blockhouse. Every obstacle has the same purpose—to delay the Viets long enough for us to rally from their little surprise!

My duty here in the blockhouse is almost at end, and I am grateful. I look forward to seeing my friends. I joke that the isolation has allowed the dreaded cafard beetle to eat most of my brain. In truth, one of the older gray-bearded men did have a fitful spell of nervous trembles before blacking out for several minutes. When his senses were restored at last, he was treated to a mug of brandy from the sergent's personal kit The troubled soldier longs to return to the village where his young *congai* waits for him.

Only the sighting of an approaching convoy breaks the monotony of blockhouse life. No one sleeps during this time so that we can watch it pass by. Sometimes, the members of the convoy will take pity on us and toss fruit or other things that we have long forgotten. Once, a passing legionnaire tossed out a box of army rations which happened to land at the feet of Sergent Cybulski. He quickly heaved it back, along with a loud vile curse that is easily recognized by any well-traveled man!

A scout vehicle, usually an armored carrier or half-track, always precedes the convoys. A small tank or another armored vehicle often follows this. The convoy itself is composed of various types of trucks and tankers loaded with men, fuel, and supplies. Additional armored vehicles and sandbagged trucks with heavy machine guns are spaced throughout the slow-moving column to add to its security. Military ambulances also take their places in the column of trucks. Merchants often travel under the protection of the military vehicles, taking their cherished goods to the depleted markets of Caobang and other remote northern settlements. The tail of a convoy disappearing from view brings no joy.

Tonight, the radio crackles with a signal from the larger blockhouse at Poste Kilometrique 59. It is a distress call! They are presently under attack and are requesting artillery fire from the long guns of a supporting base. They also ask for assistance from any aircraft that might be in the area on standby. Our rooftop sentries report hearing the distinct faint explosions coming from the general area of PK 59. The urgent broadcasts from the beleaguered outpost continue for approximately twenty minutes and then the radio becomes silent. This is bad! Following procedure, our sergent does not attempt to contact the other blockhouse. It is just as well for we have nothing to offer beyond one or two silent prayers that they be spared from suffering.

The next day, we receive no word concerning the fate of PK 59, but by eavesdropping on the radio messages of others, our sergent is able to determine that a tank force from further north of us has been sent to evaluate the situation there. It is likely that many weeks will pass before we learn the fate of the twenty men at the blockhouse just a few kilometers up the highway.

We do receive a radio message warning us to be alerted to the nearby presence of a Viet Minh regiment. Our concerned sergent feels that this is the same force that engaged our neighbor last night, and so he immediately begins preparations for the eventual defense of PK 54. First, each of us is blindfolded to simulate the dark conditions that we would be operating in during a night assault. Then, as blind men, we repeatedly drill for hours on all phases of our weapons...their working order...and the exact placements of our stores of ammunition. All useful radio frequencies are written in large numbers on a chalkboard and placed beside the radio—just in case a less experienced blockhouse member may be forced to operate it. Large wooden barrels are filled with water and then placed about the chamber. Two heavy opened crates of grenades are hoisted onto the roof, and additional rounds of illumination and high explosive shells are unpacked and made ready by the three members of the mortar crew. The bearded lovesick legionnaire and I are posted together as sentries on the roof. Hot coffee is made available to us during the night by the lowering of a bucket, which is tied to a length of cord.

It is no surprise to us that the Viets have chosen this night for their attack. It begins with the explosion of a single landmine in the field across the highway and west of the bridge. My gray-bearded partner and I fire into the darkness in that direction at two figures that seem frozen and confused following their comrade's deadly misstep. Our rifle shots alert the other legionnaires, especially the mortar team, which now fires off several illumination rounds. These ignite within seconds, flickering brightly as they float lazily over the perimeter defensives. Several landmines now explode east of the blockhouse and north of the river. My comrade and I are surprised to see a wave of advancing rebels who have already reached the barriers of tangled barbed wire. They are working feverishly to penetrate the stubborn wire. The machineguns situated on the east and west walls now begin rattling, aiming their deadly effective fire at the masses of approaching Viets. It seems obvious that their first objective tonight is the blockhouse and not the bridge. The mortar crew is now firing high explosive shells. Some of these burst with great effectiveness, while others impact harmlessly behind the Viets in areas they have already advanced through.

A scene of quiet discipline prevails within the fortified walls of the main chamber. Cybulski has calmly radioed for artillery support as well as requesting help from any planes that might be within range of the radio. The gunner, who had been previously assigned to the north wall, has taken a new position with the automatic rifle at the firing slit on the east side. Although working in total darkness, the gunners find ample targets to choose from, firing as fast as their weapons will allow. The lingering volume of acrid smoke from the traversing machine guns has nowhere to go. It begins to fill the entire room, choking the men as they desperately gasp for clean air. Suddenly, shells from the support base begin to scream in as they fall around the besieged blockhouse. Hot growling shell splinters from the artillery barrage slice through the rebel lines. Some of the artillery rounds are aimed to blast into the surrounding jungle where unseen numbers of Viets are massed, waiting as reserves for a signal to join in the final assault on the outpost.

Bullets and shell splinters whistle by as my comrade and I crouch for cover between our hurried tosses from the supply of grenades. The enemy bullets make distinct chipping sounds as they strike the concrete works just above our heads. We have already emptied the contents of one crate on the attacking Viets. Illumination rounds lighting the perimeter reveal that great numbers of them are withdrawing even though the trumpet recall has not been sounded. Many are without their weapons as they stumble away in confusion. I decide to report this bit of good news to those within the main chamber. As I open the trap door, the thick choking white smoke from the automatic guns begins to billow out from the confinement of the central chamber. Inside, I can hear the men coughing violently, gagging as their lungs scream for unspoiled air.

The column of foul smoke from the bunker's discharged weapons continues to pour from the opening as I look in to report on what we have seen from the roof. The sergent climbs the ladder and joins us on the roof where he looks out over the scene between desperate gasps for fresh air. The incredible noise inside the tight chamber has temporarily deafened him, and his watery eyes are blood red from the burning sting of the trapped smoke. When I offer him water from my canteen, he snatches it from me and quickly gulps it down, pouring the very last of it over his head and face. Then he scrambles back down through the smoke, and radios the artillery command center to request that the shelling be directed to coordinates in an area of the jungle where the remainder of the Viet regiment is either withdrawing or possibly massing for another attack. The barrage halts momentarily as an adjustment is calculated and then shells begin to slowly howl in, exploding with fiery thunder beneath the high canopy of jungle. It appears that we have prevailed in our struggle to live for another day! And there may be few because the rebels are determined men, who die much too bravely for a cause I have yet to understand. The gray-bearded legionnaire and I welcome the warmth of the morning sun, while our mysterious little foe will sit patiently—waiting for the sheltering blanket of another moonless nightfall.

The morning light brings renewed hope, but from our rooftop, a panoramic view of death surrounds us. Large black ants are already scavenging over the lifeless bodies of the fallen communists. Smoke drifts lazily upward through the canopy of the jungle forest in several places, evidence of numerous smoldering brush fires that resulted from the overnight artillery barrages. A curious young monkey has wandered out of the jungle and is playfully slapping at the ear of a dead Viet. The gray-bearded legionnaire becomes enraged and curses aloud upon seeing this. He quickly fires his rifle at the defiling little ape, but misses. His purpose is achieved, however, as the startled monkey jumps high in the air, then dashes for the safety of the forest.

Although two members of the mortar crew were slightly wounded, Sergent Cybulski reports that no one was killed. A relief column has been dispatched and will assist us with the removal and burial of the remaining enemy casualties. As is their custom, hundreds of Viet coolies have already hauled away many of their dead and wounded from the heavily cratered area surrounding the blockhouse. I am pleased that my duty here in the crypt is almost complete.

CHAPTER 13

I discover that much has changed upon my return to Phu Tong Hoa. Sergent Wimmer remains here and is now the sergent-chef, while dear friends, Guenther and Corporal Andersen, have been sent to join a battalion from the regiment at a town called Thatkhe. Vu and one other montagnard guide have also gone there. The news saddens me, but my spirit is quickly restored when I learn that I will soon report for a new assignment in Hanoi with the Regiment's medical company.

*****

Hanoi is a large frightened city of ugly buildings. Many Catholics have fled to the south, and the only remaining businesses are those which profit most from the war. The city's population is fearful that the French are slowly losing control of the frontier border with China as well as pockets of country not too distant from Hanoi. All activity in the city appears to be related to the war with the communists.

*****

For many months now, I have been working in the hospital motor pool, cleaning and maintaining the ambulances, but this week, I am happy to receive a promotion to driver. I will be driving an ambulance on the supply convoys to the garrisons from Langson north to the large city of Caobang near the Chinese border. Our maps clearly identify the highways that connect the town garrisons along the Chinese frontier.

Today, the regular medical orderly, with myself as driver, are part of the convoy traveling on Route Colonial 1 from Hanoi to the garrison at Langson. At Langson, our mile-long column continues north on the more dangerous RC 4. Recent convoys using this highway have reported crippling ambushes by well-organized troops. For this reason, we find it necessary to proceed cautiously through the numerous mountain passes. In anticipation of just such an ambush, the security vehicles bristle with readied guns. We have been assured that Legion patrols continually roam these very same mountains in search of the ambushers. As we approach Thatkhe, now home to Corporal Andersen and Guenther, I imagine the two of them presently walking in the hills that overlook this highway.

The convoy arrives in Thatkhe without interruption. I see many legionnaires from the battalion that is garrisoned here, but there is no time to look for my friends. We pause long enough to refuel, then continue on toward the next garrison at Dongkhe. High spectacular limestone cliffs now rise in view. These are strange because absolutely nothing grows on their tall peaks. Their desert-like surfaces are marked with hundreds of caves and crevices, which have been created over the centuries by dissolving pockets of lime. The barren hills remind me of the American West I saw in the Tom Mix motion pictures. We have been told to be extremely vigilant in this area as the caves make ideal places for the Viets to set up their guns.

As predicted, several shots ring out behind us further back in the column. In my imagination, I see wild, savage Indians and bloodthirsty outlaws firing at us from their hiding places in the dry high-desert mountains. The winding convoy counters with a frenzy of automatic guns and weapons, firing blindly into the cliffs in every direction. Unscathed, we continue on.

In the early afternoon, we arrive at Dongkhe, a strange little town enveloped on all sides by mountainous jungle and fortified defenses. Again, we do not linger here very long because Caobang must be reached on schedule. Soon, RC 4 becomes very narrow as it snakes and winds its way upward through the confines of the tight mountain passes. Here, the jungle provides unlimited concealment from either side of the road.

At last, we have reached Caobang, successfully traveling the 120 kilometers with no casualties. Caobang surprises me because of its tremendous size. There is much commerce. Everything can be bought here. The Chinese merchants who traveled here with the convoy today have brought many new goods for the markets of the city. Details of shirtless legionnaires from the garrison work quickly to unload their newly arrived supplies. Some of the workers jokingly remark that the convoys actually consume more fuel than they bring—a simple truth? After an overnight rest, our convoy returns to Hanoi.

*****

I have just completed my seventh convoy to Caobang. Recently, we traveled on RC 3 to Bac Kan and then further north to the garrison at Phu Tong Hoa. The Legion cemetery at Phu Tong Hoa, like French cemeteries everywhere, had grown frightfully larger. I looked for but could not find the grave of Private Lindler. I suspect that it may have been lost forever among the rows of tilting wooden crosses.

The blockhouse by the bridge at PK 54 is still manned; however, the charred concrete fortress further north at PK 59 has been abandoned since that fateful night when the radio signal from its defenders ended so abruptly. The blackened ruin sits as a sobering reminder to all who pass this way, another isolated "tomb" for the twenty legionnaires who perished there two years earlier!

*****

When I am not driving or working in the hospital motor pool, I continue my training as a medical orderly. The army nurses in the hospital are very skilled and extremely dedicated. Some are pretty and often ask me to light their English cigarettes. I always make certain that I have a good supply of matches. Greta would be surprised to know that her young brother has been shaving once a week now for almost one year. When I find it necessary to shave every day, then

I will grow a fine, handsome beard like the older men. Then I will need even more matches!

*****

The Viets have become increasingly bolder in their attacks on our convoys and northern strongholds. Rumors circulate around Hanoi that the rebels now have tens of thousands in their ranks. This is enough men for several divisions. Many are armed with automatic weapons, bazookas, and heavy guns, which have either been provided by the Chinese communists or plundered from the stores of our own fallen outposts and overwhelmed convoys. More precautions are taken on RC 4, but still the destruction continues.

*****

It is midmorning as today's heavily armed convoy snakes cautiously through another narrow winding gorge beyond Langson. My ambulance is near the center of the mile-long column when I hear a tremendous explosion. This is followed immediately by another earth-shaking blast and the unmistakable sound of many machine guns chattering away. An unseen hell has erupted at the head of our column. The convoy slows even though the radio commander urges all vehicles to continue at their present speed. As I drive beyond the bend that has been blocking our view, the medic and I see an armored car and another truck, a weapons carrier, which have struck road mines. Other trucks are attempting to pass the destroyed vehicles but cannot because of the intense machine-gun fire and rockets from the Viets' well-concealed positions in the jungle. They have staged an elaborate trap for us this morning, and we have blindly stumbled into it. I have no option but to continue driving forward into the deadly hail of fire. An exploding rocket hits another truck in front of the ambulance. It bursts into flames as several men scramble from it. They are felled almost immediately by the waiting machine gunners.

Enormous explosions are now heard coming from the rear of the stalled, confused convoy. The trap is now complete as even more hidden machine guns join the battle. Legionnaires jump from the backs of the slow-moving trucks and seek cover, but there is none. Well-aimed bullets rake every vehicle, including my ambulance, but I continue to creep forward around the burning trucks. Some dismounted men react by shooting blindly into the mountains, while others form into small groups and dash into the jungle's edge looking for their attackers. My companion jumps from the ambulance as more bullets pelt us from all directions. I notice that some trucks have actually been able to get around the blockage of burning vehicles, so I am determined to do the same. As I turn to look back, I see volleys of grenades being thrown by the Viets, who are now standing upright and advancing toward the column. There are hundreds of them. More trucks are set afire from the exploding grenades. Groups of men are firing wildly at the visible grenadetossing Viets. Even in the midst of all the confusion, some brave legionnaires are counterattacking the deadly machine guns with grenades of their own. As I drive around the burning truck, I am so close that I can feel the fire's intense heat. Suddenly a lone Viet with a rocket launcher steps out of the brush directly in front of me. He takes aim as I attempt to run him over with the ambulance. I am too late!

The impact of the blast throws me violently from my seat as the uncontrollable ambulance leaves the roadway and crashes into another burning truck. I can no longer hear the den of the raging slaughter as the rocket blast has deafened me. I crawl out on the side nearest the forest and continue crawling, hoping to reach cover without being seen. I make it a short distance into the waist-high brush when I suddenly receive a painful unexpected kick in my left shoulder. Even in my dazed state, I realize that I have not been kicked—I have been shot! I am also bleeding from the temple, which probably resulted from the explosion of the rocket. With all my remaining strength, I struggle to pull myself deeper into the grass and further away from the highway. A powerful unyielding darkness slowly overtakes me.

The pressure of busy hands on my throbbing forehead gradually awakens me. Squatting directly over me is a lone Viet medical orderly, easily recognized by the white cotton mask strapped over his nose and mouth. He has removed my shirt, shredded it into pieces, and fashioned a bandage from one sleeve, which is wrapped snuggly around my head. I am weaponless and lacking the strength and will to defend myself. The Viet signals for me to sit up, and I am able to do so with considerable pain. There is complete silence! Either the battle is now over, or I am still deaf. Both things happen to be true, however, as the orderly now sprinkles a white antiseptic powder on my injured shoulder. He rips the rest of my shirt into two pieces and then, using one piece as a bandage, he ties it securely over the blood-less wound. With the remaining piece, he fashions a sling around my neck and under my left arm to prevent me from moving it. He steps back from me momentarily to inspect his handiwork. Sitting upright causes me to black out again.

When I come to, I realize the Viet has moved me under a nearby tree and propped me up with my back against it. From this sitting position, I look around and discover that I am further away from the highway than I had imagined. I cannot see it from here, nor can I begin to sense where it might be. The orderly's gestures indicate that neither of us have any water. From around his neck, he removes a leather thong that has a slender section of hollow bamboo tied to it. This bamboo tube is plugged tightly with a crude wooden cork, which he now removes. He shakes several dry green leaves into my hand from the bamboo container and then, after removing his white mask, he smiles and motions for me to chew them. I do this and soon discover moisture returning to my extremely dry mouth. The Viet takes several leaves from the tube for himself and then hands it to me. He indicates that he wishes for me to keep the thong and its contents, for he is certain that I will need it more than he. I am con-fused by these unexpected acts of compassion and generosity from an enemy whose resources are very meager when compared to our own. He removes a folded green banana leaf from his shirt pocket and places it in my hand. I pass out again but remain upright against the tree. When I come to, I discover that nighttime is approaching, and the Viet orderly has disappeared.

My medical training indicates that I have experienced a head concussion, but I do not know the severity. Since there is only the one wound from the bullet that struck me as I fled the ambulance, it must still be lodged in my inflamed left shoulder. This would account for my burning fever. I am completely deaf and, presently, too disoriented to either stand or move in an attempt to find the roadway. My thirst seems unquenchable, but I refresh myself by chewing on one of the green leaves from the bamboo tube.

I am unable to rest during the night. A host of large mosquitoes are aggravated to a vicious frenzy by the presence of blood on my shirtless body. I become their feast! The mosquitoes work to drive me insane, but fortunately, I am not in full possession of my senses. Even in this addled condition of mind, I am still deeply puzzled by the Viet's show of kindness. Perhaps their dominance in this struggle is now so overwhelming and so obvious to them that the Viets can afford to be merciful while crushing us—and perhaps, we do not yet realize this!

At dawn, I realize that I am still clutching at the folds of banana leaf left by the Viet medic. I carefully open it and discover that it contains a small piece of wild bee honeycomb. I eat this and find my spirit and strength are slightly restored. My thirst is still very great, but I choose to save the remaining green leaves in the hollow tube since I may need them later.

I have not lost consciousness now for several hours, but my fever has increased tremendously. Although I still cannot hear a thing, I do begin to feel the ground trembling slightly. It can only be from the movement of an approaching column of tanks. Undoubtedly, the tanks and heavy recovery vehicles are just arriving to remove the abandoned and destroyed vehicles from yesterday's disaster. I know that I must make an effort to walk in their direction because they would never hear my voice above their own noisy business. I thoughtfully place the thong around my neck and rise slowly, while steadying myself against that very same tree. I am overcome with nausea and dizziness, but I allow this to pass. Although I am excited at the prospect of being rescued by the recovery detail, I do not hurry. I must stop and rest from tree to tree. This feverish exertion is painful, but I eventually reach the clearing where my stricken ambulance came to its final stop beside another disabled truck. I am startled to see that it has also been entirely consumed by flames, most likely the results of a ruptured fuel tank. It is fortunate that no one was inside when it burst into flames. I sit here and rest briefly as I survey the fire-gutted remains of my ambulance. Two helmeted crewmen jump from the nearest tank and walk cautiously toward me. One appears to be extending his canteen out to me as he approaches closer. He has a gold tooth...

The next day is April 30, 1950, and I awake in the garrison hospital at Caobang. There are several surprises as I reach my twentieth birthday and the Legion Day of the Camerone.

The greatest gift is the joy that I feel knowing that my cherished friend, Blackie, is alive and well after all! At last, I can stop worrying about him! He is now Sergent Bak, tank commander, and it was fated that he should arrive there yesterday morning as part of the recovery convoy. He has been to the hospital once for a brief visit and has promised to return when my head is clearer. There is much to talk about—Guenther, Corporal Andersen, the heroics of Sergent Wimmer at Phu Tong Hoa, as well as the unknown plight of our mutual friend, old Corporal Fulci. I hope each of them is celebrating right now...wherever they are. Perhaps, if we survive this war, there will be a joyous reunion that will bring us together again.

My next gift is the 9mm bullet that was removed from my shoulder yesterday and, later, unceremoniously tossed on my bed-sheet by the French surgeon who extracted it. He says that the Viet soldier shot me with one of our own rifles. When I tell him about the rebel orderly who befriended me, the doctor does not seem surprised. He says this is the "new" rebel doctrine—to convince the Europeans and Africans who fight for France that they are misguided, that the communists are actually benevolent and humane people. The doctor informs me that I am not the only one to have benefited from this new philosophy. It seems that others have also had similar experiences with the Viets.

He adds, "It comes straight from that bloody Mao's own field manual!"

I tell the doctor that there are more communists who would rather shoot at me than befriend me, and as long as there are, they will remain my enemy. He laughs and then informs me that the tube around my neck contained leaves from a poppy plant. He had ordered them removed earlier for analysis. My souvenir bullet fits perfectly inside the useful bamboo necklace. Two Viets, with entirely different objectives, have presented me with two birthday gifts, which I shall never forget.

The unfortunate victims of the ambushed convoy now occupy every bed in the hot overcrowded ward. Many are very quiet, while several of the more painfully wounded can be heard offering up their prayers to God and Allah or, otherwise, simply moaning in obvious personal agony. Busy hospital attendants work without rest, while the heavy unmistakable smells of blood, burned flesh, and disinfectants combine to stagnate the air. Dozens of humming wall-mounted electric fans fail in their attempts to move the fouled air from the ward. As I witness the individual degrees of physical suffering, I am grateful that my own injuries seem insignificant in comparison.

Since I am confined to the hospital ward indefinitely, I am not able to benefit from the Legion's generous tradition of work-free birthdays. Today is also the great Day of Camerone, but the ward's head nurse, a rigid, overworked nun, elects to withhold my ration of wine. She reminds me that I am recovering from a head injury, so therefore, no wine will be allowed—not even a sip! Several others in the ward do not receive this bit of news with enthusiasm, but their groans of disappointment soon subside. I do not complain as I recount the horrible misfortune on RC 4 from the comfort of my clean soft hospital bed.

After a night of rest in the Caobang hospital, my strength gradually returns, and thanks to the blessings of the new miracle drug, penicillin, I no longer have to fear the possibility of infection in my shoulder. I am declared well enough to return to Hanoi today.

Blackie has returned to the ward this morning to check on my condition, and he tells me that his tank squadron will be escorting our departing convoy halfway to Dongkhe. He looks well, although he seems to be repulsed by the sight of the breakfast food on my hospital tray. I suspect that he, like countless other legionnaires, has celebrated yesterday's festivities with far too much drink.

I eagerly share the experiences of the last four years, including those of Guenther and others from Bel Abbes. He listens with much interest and laughs when I tell him about stepping into the long-abandoned punji pit near Phu Tong Hoa. I joke with him about Vu, the smiling Meo shadow that follows me everywhere. We also laugh at Guenther and of him being unaware that Cabo Fulci's wife is a prostitute and, of course, another event of that same day, when mule-headed Blackie was resigned to eat—and enjoy—a woman's cooking! I also laugh as I tell him about the day in Saigon when I witnessed Cabo Andersen washing his stinky feet and uniform together in the same basin of water. We share another laugh at the expense of dear Corporal Andersen.

I tell him that he should be proud now that he is a sergent in the Tank Corps. He soon begins to talk freely about his adventures, and I discover that he, too, was wounded several years earlier when his tank was disabled after rolling over a large mine. On one occasion, his squadron of tanks ran low on fuel and was forced to laager near a small hamlet overnight. The Viets, hidden deep in the jungle, used a loudspeaker to keep Blackie and the other stranded legionnaires awake the entire night. The continuous broadcasts alternated between ominous threats of immediate and certain doom to kind, cheerful, persuasive offers of sanctuary for any legionnaires who might defect to their side. Blackie was amazed because every broadcast that night was delivered in German—and every crewmember of the stranded squadron, save one, was German!

Blackie is not surprised when I reveal that I have yet to be with a woman. He says there is no reason to hasten an experience that will inevitably become a physical affliction, which will drain all my resources and rob me of sound judgment. Blackie's expression is one of great despair as he reveals what he considers to be man's ultimate weakness; however, it immediately changes to one of keen interest when I mention the pretty European nurses in Hanoi. At the end of his visit to the hospital ward, Blackie reveals that he is being transferred to another tank squadron near Langson. We agree to meet again in Langson with every opportunity and to continue our earnest efforts to locate our friends. We part near Dongkhe later that day.

CHAPTER 14

The worst possible news of the war has just arrived here in Hanoi. Caobang has been completely evacuated by the French and abandoned to the Viets. During the evacuation march south through trackless jungle mountains, the entire withdrawing column of legionnaires, Moroccans, and civilians was ambushed and massacred. A full battalion of my regiment was dispatched north from Thatkhe to rendezvous with the evacuating garrison, and they, too, were destroyed...to a man. I have never prayed, but I do so now for my good friends at Thatkhe—Guenther and Corporal Andersen. Blackie remains safe as a new arrival to the detachment of Legion tanks at Langson. Since the town of Dongkhe has also fallen to the communists, they now control all of Route Coloniale 4 north from Thatkhe and the entire length of RC 3 south from Caobang, all the way to Bac Kan. Convoys will no longer be necessary to resupply the lost or evacuated French garrisons on the Chinese border.

*****

In the midst of this ordeal, I have reenlisted in the Legion for an additional five years until 1956. As promised by the Legion recruiters, I have now earned citizenship as a French national. It is doubtful, however, that this achievement will ever prove to be to my personal advantage.

*****

The fighting continues, with little progress being made by either side. We evacuate towns and then battle to retake them. After retaking the towns, we find cause to abandon them yet again. Except for two large engagements, one at Hoa Binh, and the other at Na San, we have little to encourage us. The masters of this war conceive great offensives designed to trap entire regiments, only to find that when the traps are sprung, the Viets have already fled the area ahead of them. They are careful not to engage us unless they are assured of either winning or escaping successfully. The determined Viet guerillas destroy bridges and railroads, which we rebuild, only to have them destroyed again. Lethal mines and deadly ambushes continue to take their toll on our tired, demoralized units. The Viet Minh control the countryside and receive ever-increasing support from the villagers and local population, while we must timidly withdraw into defensive positions at nightfall. The Red ants sting us repeatedly, and we continue to brush them aside. From the generals down to the privates, there is one common perception—this is a frustrating war!

There is some encouragement, however, as the French have been receiving much-needed surplus materials and equipment for over a year now from the anti-communist American government. My latest uniform has the black letters USMC stamped over the pocket. I recall the mended Italian Army overcoat I was issued over seven years ago to wear in the defense of Berlin. I also reflect on the unfortunate Italian soldier who was shot while wearing it.

Considerably more medical supplies are now being made available to the hospitals and field units. Many wounded men are already benefiting from the distribution of these needy medicines and updated medical equipment. Although small in their size, completely functioning hospitals can now be transported to areas where they are most likely to be needed. These field hospitals will save many who would otherwise die unnecessarily because of delays in their treatment.

In the cloudy gray skies Dakotas and sleek fighter-bombers are now seen flying overhead, replacing the obsolete, worn-out British and German airplanes. Determined ground crews have kept the older aircraft in service for years beyond their expected usefulness by repairing the relics with an assortment of parts scavenged from other wrecks. I recently heard that the Amis had even given a floating airplane carrier to the French Navy, and it is presently cruising offshore in the Sea of Tonkin. From there, the carrier's planes can easily reach targets anywhere in the Tonkin.

New weapons also arrive. My heavy bolt-action rifle has been replaced with a lighter rapid-firing carbine. There is also an abundance of American cigarettes, socks, chewing gum, and chocolate. The Amis have many strange, peculiar names for their products—bazookas, jeeps, napalm, Flying Boxcars, and now, a mysterious tinned meat provision called Spam. It tastes better when it is heated.

*****

Last night, while on duty at the hospital, I experienced the physical pleasure of a woman when I willingly succumbed to the lustful advances of an older nurse in a darkened supply closet. The long-anticipated experience was just as I had anticipated, except for its brevity—and my inability to walk normally for some time afterward. My physical release was immediate since I could not deny the honest joy of her hand on my sex. She is patient, however, and has graciously agreed to help me with that problem—tonight!

CHAPTER 15

I am flying in an airplane for the first time, when my medical unit is transferred to a busy new base near the tiny village of Dien Bien Phu. As our airplane circles overhead through wisps of low-hanging clouds before landing, I observe that the sprawling camp is actually composed of many separate camps scattered about on low hills in a flat plain. High mountains surround this large plain on all sides. A crewmember of the airplane tells us that we are very close to the border with Laos and indicates this by pointing out the window to the mountains that rise just west of the huge encampment.

The massive base has been constructed in this valley because there is a long-abandoned airfield here. I hear that the airfield was built and used by the Japanese during the Big War. Planes now sit, neatly parked by the airstrip. In fact, there is neatness to everything about the camp. There is another smaller landing strip located four or five kilometers south of the main camp.

The camp is very near several busy infiltration routes, which the Vietminh are currently using to bring supplies and men into the northern region from both Laos and China A small portable bridge can be seen spanning the tiny winding river that runs directly through the valley. Thousands of soldiers—Thais, Moroccans, Vietnamese, Algerians, Senegalese, French, and Legionnaires from units throughout Indochina—now man the entrenched strongpoints on the smaller hills that surround the airfield and command head-quarters. Because of its distance from Hanoi and the absence of any functional roads, the large camp's needs must be completely supplied by air. Heavy artillery pieces, and even tanks, have been flown in to support this bold offensive.

Since the southernmost base to which I have been assigned is developing a look of permanency about it, it will likely be my home for some time. My sound recollections indicate that, in three short weeks, Legionnaire No. 494321 will be celebrating his seventh Christmas in this forbidden country at the strongpoint, which has been curiously named Isabelle.

*****

I am excited when I learn that a veteran battalion from my regiment is garrisoned at Isabelle. While in conversation with legionnaires from one of the companies in the regiment, I hear a remarkable tale about a legendary old corporal who is never allowed to participate on missions outside the encampment because his body's extraordinary stench would be certain to alert the Viets, who have long been known for their keen sense of smell. I know of only one corporal in the entire Foreign Legion who has achieved such a dubious reputation—Cabo Andersen! Is it possible that my prayers were heeded, and he had somehow avoided the Thatkhe massacre three years ago? I now feel renewed in my efforts to find him. And if he is alive, then perhaps Guenther is as well? After all, they were transferred to Thatkhe in the same movement by the same directive from the regiment. To lose hope is to admit their deaths, and I will never do that.

*****

Our commander, Colonel Perrin, is an old veteran of the first big war in France. He has demanded that our bunkers and their connecting systems of trenches be constructed to withstand a pounding from big guns, even though the Viets are not likely to have them. The colonel's obsession is a result of his firsthand experiences on the battlefields of Europe when, during a massive artillery bombardment, he witnessed men being buried alive by the collapse of their poorly constructed earthworks. He is very vocal and has scoffed at the other strongpoint commanders for laxness in the preparation of their fortifications. They laugh at him behind his back, saying that this is a great waste of time and resources because the Viets could never transport big guns through the roadless jungle mountains.

Our time is certainly not wasted. We continuously dig deeper into the earth while hauling timbers from the forest to support the walls and roofs of our shelters. The colonel personally supervises our progress as Christmas Eve nears. Our deep trenches slowly become networks of fire bays, traverses, and rifle pits. Listening posts, which are large enough for two or three men at a time, extend out from the main trenches in every direction. The supply of barbed wire is limited and in great demand everywhere. For that reason, we must resort to using sharpened bamboo stakes as at Phu Tong Hoa and elsewhere.

*****

The winter monsoon season is slowly arriving. Brief torrents of rain dampen our trenches, but not our spirits as there is still much to enjoy. The beer and wine rations are issued with reliability, and we anticipate they will be increased during the coming celebration of Christmas. I hear there is even a brothel at the main camp, completely staffed by women from a region east of Bel Abbes. For those of religious faith, the Legion has provided two clergymen to live at Isabelle, where they will conduct last rites and Christian burials if necessary. Hundreds of soldiers have already joined together under the thundering rumble of heavy guns to participate in Communion Mass services.

Although we have a functional infirmary with doctors, there is a larger well-equipped underground hospital at the central stronghold. Serious medical cases will be flown to the hospital in Hanoi on one of several C-47 Dakotas, which have been converted into air ambulances. Today, in the only ambulance truck at Isabelle, I have already transported two legionnaires and a Moroccan rifleman to the underground hospital for treatment of injuries that were sustained in separate accidents. The Moroccan lost an eye while fighting with knives with one of his countrymen. He will be flown to Hanoi tomorrow.

Tonight, I will think of Christmas as I occupy a rifle pit that faces out toward the shallow river.

*****

Although our officers refuse to disclose any information concerning the situation here, all rumors indicate that we are now completely encircled by the Vietminh—perhaps by as many as three entire divisions. The enemy has taken great care to hide his presence from the constant flights of the small observation planes, knowing that detection would alert the French artillery batteries and, even worse, aircraft with their loads of the horribly feared jelly fire—napalm. Cooking fires for their rice rations are not allowed since even the smallest wisps of smoke might be detected as they rise above the jungle's treetops. Every sortie that ventures out from Dien Bien Phu in any direction meets fierce resistance and is eventually forced back by large numbers of Viet Minh soldiers. If we are indeed surrounded, then the enemy will be foolish to attack us because of our heavy guns, tanks, fighter-bombers, and excellent morale.

*****

Cold weather lingers in the valley and, with it, the early morning *crachin*. This impenetrable fog hangs unforgivingly, encompassing the entire length of the Dien Bien Phu valley plain and mountain gaps. These low-hanging mists completely hide the secretive movements of the Viets, who have thus far remained silent, except for their cautious nightly probes of our defenses. Often, the airfields remain closed for landings in the earlier hours of the day since the ground is not visible to approaching aircraft. A clever method has been devised, however, for allowing arriving transports to drop necessities by parachute with considerable accuracy. Weather balloons, filled with helium and tethered by a long cord, are released to float where they can be seen high above the foggy cloud cover. This lets the aircraft crew know exactly where to release their cargo parachutes even though they cannot see the actual drop zone. So far, this procedure has worked effectively whenever it has been necessary to use it.

*****

The Viet's long-anticipated attack has begun this afternoon at 1700 hours—and with great surprise! The communist rebels begin pounding the airfields and strong points with heavy mortars and artillery pieces that rival our own. The commanders at Headquarters are startled at first by this discovery, but they tell the junior officers not to fret because the Viets will soon run out of ammunition for their big guns. After all, they have neither the roads nor the trucks to deliver enough artillery shells to continue the tremendous bombardment that we are now receiving.

The barrage is unrelenting! It continues with great accuracy, destroying all but the sturdiest of bunkers. Two fighter planes parked at the end of the runway are suddenly hit and explode into huge fireballs. Thick black smoke boils violently from the burning wreckage. The steel matting sections that form the runway are blasted into jagged, crumpled shards of useless metal. Direct hits by the heavy guns on shelters send timbers, earth, and bits of men flying in all directions. I witness another aircraft, an observation plane, being struck by the Viets' artillery. The small spotter plane is flipped over on its back, with both wings sheared off by the force of the tremendous blast. It has not been set ablaze. Another shell destroys the main control tower and its signal beacon just as three undamaged fighter planes somehow manage to lift off safely from the severely shell-cratered runway. A distant earth-shaking blast can only mean one thing—the Viets have scored a direct hit on one of the main stronghold's ammunition depots five kilometers north of here. Nothing less than a volcanic eruption could possibly account for an explosion of that magnitude.

The deadly barrage mercifully comes to an end. I calculate that while I have been crouching in a deep hole within my bunker for the last two hours, the Viets have fired thousands of shells into the valley. Did they stop because they have exhausted their supply? I do not think so! I think that they stopped because their gunners are just simply tired and need to rest from the unmerciful beating they have just given us. Their guns now dominate the entire valley bowl from their concealed vantage points high in the surrounding hills and mountains. Even a general would admit that this situation could very well prove to be disastrous, but unfortunately, there is not a single one to be found anywhere in the valley.

A week passes, with Isabelle being shelled at random intervals, but I learn that things are much worse for the other strong points outlying the command center. Several have been completely overrun by masses of well-trained, highly motivated Vietminh regulars! The few defenders who were not killed in the onslaughts managed to escape to other several hundred strongholds, yet many have chosen to flee the fight altogether. T'ai and Colonial conscripts have thrown down their weapons and taken refuge near the river, away from encampments that are still bravely resisting the communists. These deserting "river rats" rush out during the parachute supply drops and make off with provisions that are intended for those of us who continue to hold on. Although it is tempting to do so, our NCOs order us not to shoot at the miserable thieving cowards. Oddly enough, the Viets do not fire at them either, perhaps because they have concluded that these dogs no longer present a threat to them anymore.

*****

Many of the surviving defenders of the fallen strongholds have arrived at Isabelle to help strengthen our defenses and replace our own casualties. I look on as they stagger into our camp in small demoralized groups that now represent all that remains of their original units. Two dejected faces do not go unnoticed! It is Guenther, as well as Corporal Andersen, walking by with fixed, straightforward gazes…but seeing nothing. I hesitate to call out because I am disturbed by the solemn, trance-like processional passing before me. But being moved to act before it is too late, I shout out their names.

"Private Dern… Cabo Andersen… Look this way! It is I… Dieter Koob!"

Their heads slowly turn in my direction as they hear their names being shouted aloud unexpectedly. As I approach the two men, their faces suddenly beam with surprised delight. They seem to recognize me immediately—even after a separation of almost five years! It is a wonderful, special moment as we embrace as dear friends who have finally been reunited.

My haggard comrades have not yet fully recovered from the ordeal of last week when their positions were stormed and overrun by swarms of Viets. In an organized withdrawal, they were able to fight their way through the attackers and make it safely to another stronghold. Both have earned promotions while garrisoned at Thatkhe. Guenther is now a corporal, while Legionnaire Andersen has been promoted to sergent. I also learn that each of them has enlisted for an additional five years in the Legion. They listen with interest as I disclose the circumstances of my encounter with Blackie, and I listen with equal interest as they recall their personal adventures and many narrow escapes from certain death at the hands of the well-organized Viet Minh regiments near Thatkhe. We all agree that much uncertainty surrounds us here in this valley, but nonetheless, our spirits are greatly restored by this chance encounter today. I sense that there is still much fight left in these old survivors who would rather "die well than live badly." Even as another murderous nighttime barrage befalls a distant friendly outpost, I sleep soundly, knowing my friends are safe and a reluctant believer's first and only prayer has been answered.

CHAPTER 16

A Dakota air ambulance, identified by the bold red crosses painted on either side of the fuselage, sits with its engines idling, waiting for the last of the wounded to be loaded from my ambulance truck. As I struggle to assist an amputee who is having difficulty boarding the plane, an artillery shell destroys my truck, while killing the two air ambulance orderlies who were busy removing the last of the litter cases from Isabelle. The tremendous explosion also kills the wounded legionnaire on the litter. Since there is no one else to care for the two dozen men who have already been loaded onto the plane, the medical evacuation officer orders me to jump on at the last possible moment. I scramble on just as other shells begin to fall onto the airstrip. A crewmember secures the door as the plane races down the runway. As we lift off and rise higher to clear the ring of mountains, flak shells burst in the air all around us. Some of the bursts are close enough to send a slight shudder through the length of the straining Dakota, but it continues rising until we reach a safer altitude. The dangers of Dien Bien Phu are now far below us. I am prevented from looking through a window because the wounded here represent those with the most extreme injuries in the entire garrison. For the next hour, the medical officer, a female air nurse, and myself tend to the immediate needs of every man as best we can in the overcrowded aircraft. Dirty blood-soaked dressings are replaced with clean ones found stored onboard with other medical supplies.

Three of the twenty-five men die from their wounds on the air ambulance before we land over one hour later at the Gia-Lam airfield near Hanoi. Their bodies are removed last so that those who have a chance of surviving can receive attention as soon as possible. I am ordered to remain with the plane to assist with its scrubbing and disinfecting after all the wounded and dead have been removed.

The airport is a busy center of activity. Planes bound for Dien Bien Phu are constantly taking to the skies, while others are either being loaded with cargo or rearmed with bombs and munitions. A squadron of newly arriving Flying Boxcars lands nearby. The deafening noise from their powerful engines makes conversation impossible. Since I am here as a result of a direct order and the unexpected deaths of the two air-taxi medical orderlies, I must report to my unit at the Hanoi military hospital. After catching a ride from the airfield on an empty weapons carrier, I arrive and recount the day's events to the duty NCO.

He laughs when I tell him that I must return to Dien Bien Phu as soon as it can be arranged. "As of today, there will be no more planes sacrificed on the landing strips of that hellhole! Sixteen planes have been destroyed or put out of action on those airfields— and that includes the two that were lost there today!" The sergent hesitates for a moment. "The only way you will ever return to that god-forsaken piece of land is by parachute. They must be desperate for replacements there too because a directive has just been issued by Headquarters that will now allow men to jump into that pit without parachutist credentials or experience." He paused again. "You just came from there...is it really the bloody mess we hear it is?"

I thought for a moment and then answered. "Well, it does look bad, but I think we will eventually prevail."

Then the sergent adds. "I hear the Viets are being killed by the hundreds. Are they that easy to kill?" He smirked as he waited for my answer. As I had just hosed the blood of twenty unfortunate men from the bay of the Dakota ambulance, I did not wish to continue on the subject.

"Yes!" I respond defiantly. "They are very easy to kill, but then, so are we!" I excuse myself to shower, soupe, and visit briefly with my appreciative nurse-friend at the hospital. The duty sergent's information was correct, but I am determined to rejoin Guenther and Sergent Andersen. After all, it took me five incredibly long years to find them.

Today, I make my way to the deployment station where I add my name to the growing list of volunteers who have chosen to jump out of an airplane for the first time in their lives. Many have arrived before me. Each volunteer has already heard the horrible stories that have filtered back to Hanoi—openly exposed parachutists being shot in the air as they float down above Dien Bien Phu, others being knifed unexpectedly by throngs of waiting Viets as soon as they touch the ground, miscalculations that deposit the jumpers in deadly minefields or barbed wire entanglements, and the exhilarating jumps made at night into the unknown darkness below. My reasons for jumping are known only to me, and I do not regret that decision, but what of the others? What motivates these men? Could it be the adventure they seek? Or a sense of duty? Or perhaps, the justification of knowing that one died well for a cause of one's own choosing—a purposeful death triumphing over a meaningless one! I will never know what brings us together to take this unimaginable risk, but I intend to survive and rejoin the only friends I have.

As I leave the hospital tonight, I hear a very familiar expression being repeated in a very familiar voice. "You same children! Children same you!" It can only be Vu, the raw-frog eating Meo tribesman from our days together at the village of Phu Tong Hoa. I turn to greet his predictable big smile with one of my own. We stand there looking at each other silently, smiling, still unable to communicate much beyond some recognizable hand and body gestures. One thing is obvious about Vu—he is a truly happy man. I encourage him to walk with me back to my barracks, and once there, I notice a military insignia patch on his shirt that indicates he is a member of my regiment's reconnaissance platoon. It is a difficult task, but with the aid of a map and pen and paper, I am able to explain to Vu my intent to parachute into Dien Bien Phu. He does not seem pleased by the idea of jumping from an airplane. Using the same map and pen, Vu is able to let me know that he has just returned from an extended leave of several years to visit his home and family in the highest mountains of northern Laos. We drink several bottles of beer before I succumb to a deep sleep.

Today begins! As ordered, I report to Field 19 at the Hanoi airfield for several hours of mandatory parachute training. Here, in a remote field overgrown with tall grass, sit rows of wrecked air transports, each without wings—C-47s and Flying Boxcars from America and a British Bristol (their fuselages riddled by antiaircraft fire), oil-splattered German Junkers, and other worn-out relics from the Big War.

Two hundred men crowd alongside me this cool gray morning in this graveyard of wingless aircraft. The majority of the volunteers are German-speaking legionnaires like me, but many others are from distinguished units of the Algerian and Moroccan Rifles. Senegalese artillerymen sit quietly, alone in a circle, while small groups of Thai and Vietnamese scouts are seen squatting patiently under the fuselage of a dead Dakota. Vu rises unexpectedly from their gathering place and walks toward me, smiling! I am greatly surprised to see him here! In his hand, he clutches my pen and my paper as well as the map from last night's "conversation." The smiling little man from the mountains has decided to jump with me!

The surprises continue! I can scarcely recognize an older, frail Cabo Fulci as he walks directly toward me, his manners obviously weakened by that devil-ridden yellow scourge—malaria! It is a long embrace with my teacher from the regiment at Bel Abbes—our regiment, the same one with two battalions still holding fast at Dien Bien Phu! He has also volunteered to jump. Cabo Fulci says that he is jumping because there are at least three men in Dien Bien Phu, maybe four, who would be willing to stand over his grave after he is dead and buried under the ground.

"A life is wasted unless there are at least three men, good or bad, gathered there to truly mourn your passing," he says, adding, "unless, of course, prevailing circumstances deem it to be otherwise." He is surprised to see me in Hanoi as I am one of the four he knew for sure to be in Dien Bien Phu. I explain how I came to be here now.

I also explain to Corporal Fulci that Vu will also be parachuting with me tomorrow into Isabelle, where Guenther and Sergent Andersen are now posted. He says that we must stay close together because if we train together today, then we will jump together tomorrow.

He likes the name… Isabelle.

The paratroop instructors divide the two hundred of us into twelve man groups called sticks. As this is being done, Fulci and I seize Vu around his back and shoulders as we surge forward together to assure our places in the same stick. Our instructor, a sergent from the Battalion of Legion Paratroops, marches us over to the wrecked hulk of a Dakota transport. After a brief inspection, he places each of us in the order of our perceived weight, with the smallest man, Vu, being first. Next, he assigns a number to everyone in the stick. Vu is number one, Fulci number four; I am number ten. The sergent warns us to listen carefully because we will jump in this same order tomorrow morning. He explains that the lighter jumpers must leave the plane first because they sometimes drift further outside the drop area than do the heavier men.

The instructor pauses to verify the names on the training roster. Corporal Fulci and I are rightly concerned about the added danger that the unsuspecting little montagnard might encounter because of his slight body. Fulci has a plan! Excitedly, he suggests having Vu jump tomorrow while wearing an additional pack. He says the extra pack could even be filled with special goods and surprises for our unsuspecting brothers at Dien Bien Phu. He remarks that the added weight would certainly be to my little friend's advantage. The old corporal, pausing to collect himself after a mild fit of malaria-induced shivering, inserts this for thought. "An old muleskinner like me can pack him just right so he won't lame up or break his ankles if he lands badly. For all we know, the weight of our generosity might just save his life!" We agree to talk more after training.

The parachute instructor addresses us. "You are scheduled to jump tomorrow morning, from an altitude of 600 feet. There are two advantages here for you! First of all, this is an excellent time of day to jump because the *crachin* will be thick enough to conceal you from the Vietminh gunners once you are on the ground. Secondly, you will not be exposed to their guns as long by jumping from the low altitude. Today, we will teach each of you more than you will actually need to know to make one successful parachute jump. It need not be your last one if you listen carefully and always look me in the eyes. And do not worry, if you should freeze up in the door tomorrow morning over Dien Bien Phu, myself, or someone larger than me, will be there to kick you out!"

Each member of our stick is issued a repacked main chute and an auxiliary chute, along with a sturdy well-used harness. According to the instructor, our parachutes have already been tested several times before in the skies over Dien Bien Phu. In actual fact, he claims that most of the equipment assigned to our stick has been recovered and returned from the battle three times already.

Once the gear is properly assembled and carefully inspected, the sergent demonstrates the correct way to strap it on. By working in teams of two, we are able to manage the needed adjustments and then, when satisfied that all is in order, we standby until another inspection is made. We are instructed to wear the bulky parachutes until our training is completed later this morning.

As we climb aboard the narrow fuselage of a wrecked C-47 to become familiar with the jumpmaster's commands, some wrestle awkwardly with their cumbersome packs which keep them off balance. Others accidentally slam their packs abruptly into other struggling trainees, who respond with well-aimed threats and curses. In a short time, everyone adjusts to the confining space of the Dakota's interior, and we take our seats in the already-established jumping order. The commands are simple for everyone—except Vu. For him, the sergent demonstrates.

"Stand up!" We stand.

"Hook up!" We comply by pretending to clip our main chute's release cord to the overhead anchor line. Tomorrow morning, we will not pretend. Before the last command is issued, the instructor stops to first demonstrate the correct body position for landing.

"Keep your legs and feet tightly together after you leave the plane. As you see the ground come up to meet you, relax your body and bend your knees very slightly to cushion the impact of landing." He adds, "Your ankles may be sore or swollen for a few days afterward, but otherwise, do not worry about them. Now watch me!" He stands in the center of the doorway, with his arms out and his hands firmly gripping both sides of the open door. Then from an altitude of six feet, he pushes himself out through the open door, hitting the ground with his feet together and his knees bent as instructed. Vu is watching closely as the paratrooper recovers by immediately springing back to an upright position. "Go!" On this command, Number One jumps as everyone moves up one position in the plane. When the command "Go!" is repeated by the jumpmaster, the second man jumps, and again each of us moves up another position. This sequence of "Go!" commands continues until the last member of the stick has jumped and then we climb back into the wreck and do it all over again—many times.

"Stand up!" "Hook up!"

"Go!"

The sergent seems to be satisfied as we progress through the orientation. He instructs us to remove the parachutes.

"Report to the Paras Hangar in the morning at 0300 hours for a proper fitting and last rehearsal. You must bring your own weapons and ammunition as well as your personal kits. We do not have paratrooper boots for you, so you must wear your regular ones. Take a hammer and drive all the boot nails in as far as they will go. This will help in preventing you from slipping on your plane's metal floor. I also recommend that you make room in your packs for some strong spirits, plenty of waterproof matches, lots of coffee, fresh fruit, dry cigarettes and, last of all, signed and witnessed papers attesting to be your last wills!" Some of us find this to be humorous and laugh—others do not! The instructor continues. "All of the instructors here at Gia-Lam airfield respect what you have chosen to do. We also have comrades at Dien Bien Phu, and when our job is finished, we will be joining with them as you are doing tomorrow morning. Now spend the rest of the day attending to your affairs and getting your gear in proper order. Sleep well tonight since it may be your last rest for a while. You are dismissed!"

With faithful Vu following, Corporal Fulci and I head for the base canteen. It is already crowded even though it is only midday. I tell Fulci that he could have avoided the malaria bug if only he had consumed more alcohol. He responds by saying that he had sworn off all drink in an effort to stay faithful to his dear wife, Samira. However, when he wrote to tell her that he had been obligated to reenlist in the Legion for an additional five years, she denounced him and their blissful marriage by telling him to go to hell! He has not heard from her since. He strongly suspects that she is being unfaithful. Poor Cabo Fulci. At least, he is now free to have several beers with us.

We talk excitedly about the possibility of joining our friends once again and how surprised they will be to see the three of us. Meanwhile, Vu is unaware that Fulci and I are scheming to overload his pack tomorrow for his own good. We finish our beers, realizing that there is much more that has to be done before morning. We separate until then. On the way back to my company, I make two worthwhile stops—one at the commissary and one at the mess hall kitchen.

Morning. Cabo Fulci and Vu are waiting for me when I arrive at the Paras Hangar. Their smiling faces welcome me. As planned, the clever Fulci has brought along another pack for Vu to jump with. It is filled entirely with bottles of rum and brandy, each being carefully padded with Fulci's uniforms to reduce breakage. The old corporal is obviously pleased with his creation. I, too, have an additional pack, which contains three-dozen fresh oranges, ten cans of Spam and a replenished aid kit.

I hand it to Fulci, explaining, "Yesterday, I noticed that you have lost much weight during your battle with malaria. This twenty-five-pound pack, my friend, is for you! And now all of us can jump safely and without worry." Fulci laughs and then nods approvingly. We secure the additional loads.

The hangar crews fit us with our chutes, making certain that they are adjusted properly for each jumper. We board one of four idle Dakotas that have been designated to drop replacements for the garrison at Isabelle. As we take off in the morning darkness, the jumpmaster tells us to relax because we will not reach Dien Bien Phu valley for another ninety minutes. He warns that we will have to jump very quickly once we approach Isabelle because the aircraft will only be over the small camp's dropping zone for a few seconds. The words of caution are lost on Vu, but since he will be the very first to jump, it is of little importance. Then the jumpmaster surprises every-one by producing an unopened bottle of rum which he has brought along for our enjoyment. The bottle is quickly emptied after several passes around the bay. I am nervous. The business before us is most dangerous.

As we approach the valley for our jump into darkness, the noise of the planes' powerful engines has alerted the Vietminh gunners. At this point, everything begins to happen very quickly. Even though we cannot hear the jumpmaster's voice above the roar of the engines and the air rushing through the open door, we are able to follow his visual signals. A light directly over the cockpit door begins to blink steadily.

"Stand up!"

"Hook up!" Then we wait for that last, final command that will send each of us falling helplessly to the uncertainties below. Little Vu stands before the open door, looking downward and, understand-ably, for this lone occasion, he is not smiling.

"Go!" The brave montagnard jumps without hesitation.

This is followed immediately in rapid succession, "Go… Go… Go!" There goes Corporal Fulci! Finally, I am before the open door! "Go!" I leap out, dropping fast like a heavy stone. Suddenly, the para-chute opens fully. A terrific jolt snatches me upward briefly as the rate of my descent is shockingly reduced. The early morning crachin covers the valley just as the instructor had predicted. As I float down to meet it, the enemy guns are busy. Some have targeted our planes, which by now are rising safely out of the valley. Others fire wildly at us from all directions as we drift downward, their streaking white tracers lighting up the darkness above the blanket of gray mist. Loud booms from the Viet artillery can now also be heard as they begin to fire blindly into the unseen drop area beneath the crachin. As I enter the fog, I prepare for the impact of landing. I do not have to wait long as I hit the ground with such force that I am toppled over. As I struggle to stand, I am surprised by the heat rising from the ground all around me. I suddenly realize that I have rolled into a smoking shell crater. I also realize that I would be dead if I had landed in this same spot one minute earlier. I gather my chute and release the harness before deciding to run in the direction of the friendly 155mm batteries of Isabelle. There is no time now to search out my companions because the Viet shells are beginning to land dangerously close. Our fates are now in the hands of the stronghold's recovery teams which have been dispatched to guide us back through the barbed wire and minefields.

I join Vu and Fulci after the recovery teams regroup to lead us safely inside the encampment. Miraculously, not one volunteer from the four Dakota transports has been lost or injured during the jump. However, three men have been seriously wounded by shell splinters and must be assisted back into Isabelle. Not only are Fulci and Vu safe, but their packs have also survived the jump.

Later in the week after reporting for our assignments, the three of us are able to find Guenther and Sergent Andersen sleeping in their dugout on the edge of a swampy marsh. Naturally, they are surprised and shocked to see their old friend, Cabo Fulci, as well as Vu and I. Both men have adjusted well since their narrow escape from death in that first night of battle. They are pleased to tell us that Blackie is also somewhere at Isabelle. His tank was one of two that fought their way south earlier in the week before the Viets could complete their encirclement of the camp. They have spoken to him only once but agree that anyone with a tank should not be too difficult to find again.

Fulci produces a bottle of brandy, some oranges, and two tins of Spam for our grateful friends, while Vu offers them several packs of cigarettes, pipe tobacco, and a bottle of insect repellent. Sergent Andersen insists that we open the brandy now, and no one objects. It is a fine reunion!

CHAPTER 17

The situation at Isabelle is critical. The Viet guns have destroyed several of our big guns and a munitions stockpile. An entire enemy regiment now blocks the only road from here to the main outpost, and every attempt to pass through it has met with disaster. The enemy has cleverly replaced their weapons with picks and shovels. Day and night, they can be heard busily digging deep trenches that slowly inch their way under the barbed wire and closer to our lines. The continuous heavy clouds and rain conceal the determined diggers from the fighter-bombers overhead. Every night, under cover of darkness, our patrols venture out to attack the Viet sappers and destroy their new trenches with explosives. These daring raids add to our mounting casualties, but they do very little to slow the progress of their relentless digging. Isabelle and the other camps are now surrounded and completely on their own. Every essential item, whether it is bullets, munitions, medicine, or food, must be parachuted in large quantities if we are to survive and continue fighting. The problem becomes greater when positions in the valley are lost to the Viets. As our perimeters become smaller, so do the dropping zones. The supply transports are already forced to drop their cargo from higher altitudes to avoid the surprising effectiveness of the antiaircraft fire. These factors cause many supplies to miss their intended zones altogether. Some of the parachuted cargoes fall into no man's land, where recovery is either impossible or very dangerous. Some supplies land directly in the hands of the grateful Viets. On one occasion, the rebels recovered an entire drop of 105mm shells, and they were promptly used against us.

What remains of our regiment's decimated battalion is being consolidated and positioned to defend the weakest area of the camp.

Although we are assigned to different companies, Vu and all of my comrades from Bel Abbes find ourselves squeezed into a swampy finger of land that has become a favorite target for the Vietminh artillery. Thick sticky mud created by the heavy monsoon rains is at least a foot deep in the bottom of the trenches and dugouts. The soupy mixture makes walking even a short distance very difficult. Many dirt bunkers and unsupported shelters have either collapsed or disintegrated in the continuous rains.

Blackie's lone tank is now all that remains of his original squadron. I have seen it being used repeatedly in support of the many raids on the trench-digging Viets. During a morning lull, when the Viets routinely stop fighting long enough to eat their main meal of the day, I approach him and his crew with the last remaining bottle of rum. He is happy to see me. His exhausted crew is thankful when I present them with a gift of the rum and an unopened package of cigarettes. When they are not looking, I hand Blackie the last tin of Spam and two very overripe oranges. He listens in disbelief when I tell of parachuting into Isabelle with old Fulci and Vu. He also laughs aloud upon hearing the news of Fulci's doomed marriage. Blackie must leave now. He and the crew chug off as the shelling resumes, an indication that the Viet gunners have now been fed.

The shelling continues with little respite. It would seem that the Viets would eventually expend their entire store of munitions, but that does not happen. Where do their shells come from—China? We must be at least one hundred kilometers from China—and that would be through the thick jungles of the mountains. It would seem impossible to be able to transport large loads of heavy shells over such a great distance in those conditions.

A direct hit on the dugout would certainly destroy it, but we have taken great care to conceal it from the enemy observers. We have even created an opening from the trench to the underground shelter that allows us to pass back and forth without being seen by their spotters. The random shell bursts kill or cripple many men who have no time to find shelter.

*****

The huge Packett transports appear high in the afternoon sky. We watch eagerly from the trenches as the cargo parachutes open one by one, and the much-needed supplies float down. We are sorry to see our drop of food rations, ammunitions, and medical supplies being dropped in error to smiling Vietminh coolies waiting in the surrounding jungle.

Several loads of wine narrowly miss the waiting Viets. These fall into an area known as no man's land. Another single crate, marked with the identifying red cross of the army medical services, lands alongside the only surviving load of wine and French Army bread.

It will require six men moving quickly to remove and haul away as much as possible from the three crates before the communists reach them. It will also require six additional men to advance before these as security. I hastily summon eleven other fit and willing legionnaires from the trench—with the sergent's full blessing. We waste little time passing through the now familiar minefield and then locating gaps in the coils of barbed wire.

Care is taken to remain as distant as possible from the many irretrievable bodies. The stench of death lingers heaviest there. The heavily armed squad ventures out just ahead of myself and the other five porters. We successfully reach the empty Viet trenches just as their gunners spot us closing in to retrieve some of the cargo. Their shells send us diving for the temporary safety of the muddy trench floor. As we near the stranded crates, there is an exchange of rifle fire in the trench between our security and a group of startled Viet infantry. Two smoke grenades explode as we scramble out of the enemy trench and dash for the wooden crates. A few shots are directed our way as we quickly cut away the lashings, and open each crate with metal pry bars. My partner and I quickly tear into the medical supplies, removing all that we can possibly carry back through the trenches. The others load themselves with manageable amounts of bread and wine, and then wait anxiously for the signal from the security detail. There! It is given! We run madly for our lines as wild bullets whine overhead. I glance back in time to see the security squad rapidly overtaking us in their mad dash to safety. We slide into our muddy trenches, thankful that everyone made it back safely. Vu and I set out immediately to deliver the recovered medicines to the aid station in the central bunker. The staff there is grateful for the salvaged penicillin and morphia. My fellow legionnaires are grateful for the taste of bread and wine.

CHAPTER 18

The rains have stopped for the night, and the rebels are not deterred from trenching in the muddy soil. As we listen to the busy picks and shovels working in the darkness, we hear something else. An electric loudspeaker has been moved to one of the trenches facing our position. A booming voice says, in German, "Why should you fight for France? We will reunite you with your families and comrades in East Germany. Lay down your weapons now or die in these miserable conditions!"

After a pause, the voice speaks again, only this time, in French. "Dogs of France, it is too late for you. Dien Bien Phu will be your muddy grave!"

After another pause, the message is now in Vietnamese. "Sons of Vietnam—"

This particular message is abruptly interrupted by the sounds of two exploding grenades accurately thrown by two legionnaires who had been waiting, unnoticed, in a nearby listening post. It is quiet once again.

Not a single pick or shovel can be heard again until first light. It is then that the little ants decide to continue with their digging. The morning skies are clear as the loud French Navy planes roar by our dugouts. This unexpected good weather has given their aircraft the opportunity to fly missions again. The first low-flying planes into the valley attract fire from numerous well-camouflaged antiaircraft guns. This wave of decoys is followed at a distance by a squadron of fighter-bombers hoping to spot any telltale signs of the well-hidden Viet guns. As predicted, the enemy guns begin to rattle into action as even more planes now appear to them. Hundreds of streaking white tracers from the communist guns follow the attacking Navy fighter-bombers as they roar swiftly by in search of targets for their heavy bombs and rockets. Several of the giant bombs shake the trenches upon impact.

As the menacing machine-gun duel between the Navy pilots and the Viets rages violently all around, I enter the dugout to avoid being struck by any stray bullets. Loosened dirt falls from the shelter's ceiling rafters as two of the earth-shaking heavy bombs explode among an undetermined number of enemy sappers. During this assault from the air, the undeterred siege-trenchers continue forward with their business of digging. Many of the Viet sappers are doomed, however, as the lone circling observation plane notices their activity and radios the bombers to attack the trench-works with the heavy bombs. The big bombs pound the ground with such fury that many of the enemies' trenches begin to collapse.

From the shelter of my dugout, I can see that the heavy bombing of the trenches has stopped. The Navy flyers have no more large bombs, yet their powerful droning engines can still be heard as they fly dangerously low over abandoned rice paddies. The four fighter-bombers are now using their rockets and machine guns in separate attacks against teams of Viet infantry that have been sighted in the open trenches. The luck of the daring pilots continues to hold as their planes race unscathed through the barrage of wild gunfire.

Legionnaires, many of whom have been sucked down to their knees in trench mud, loudly cheer the brave pilots on. Suddenly, as I emerge from the dugout to witness the battle, two aircrafts are struck by accurate bursts of flak. One of the damaged fighter-bombers pulls slowly away, with its lone engine sputtering wildly. This plane disappears from the valley.

The other flyer struggles valiantly to keep his plane aloft as a trail of smoke now begins to stream from its powerful but obviously crippled engine. The aircraft coughs briefly as if thirsty for more fuel and then begins a rapid climb to give the pilot enough altitude for a proper parachute jump. His aircraft is now lost and must be abandoned.

Vu and I look up as the pilot is catapulted into the air high above his doomed fighterbomber. His chute opens completely, and within seconds, the flyer tumbles down, rolling hard upon hitting the ground. His unmanned plane explodes with a deafening roar as it crashes into the mountainside. As he struggles with the chute's harness, I spot two parties of Viet riflemen converging quickly toward him from different directions. The pilot has apparently injured himself upon landing. He is clutching his right knee as he attempts to stand. His surplus of good luck appears to be exhausted at last. Vu, also aware of the enemy's presence, is excited as he points in their direction.

Suddenly, a lone fighter-bomber returns to the valley in its search for the other aircraft and their crews. The returning pilot is quick to notice the Viets rapidly closing in on his downed comrade. It appears that they wish to capture the pilot alive since he is an easy target for their riflemen. The confused communists scatter as the Navy pilot circles and then dives sharply at them, strafing the muddy flats with rockets and machine guns. His deadly fire completely disrupts the Viets, forcing them to flee back to the protection of their trenches. Streams of antiaircraft fire from the persistent Viet guns follow the lone attacking flyer as it circles for another pass in support of the downed flyer.

If the injured pilot is to be saved from capture, we must move quickly! I leap from the trench, knowing that faithful Vu is following closely behind. The network of shallow intersecting trenches slows our progress. The smell from the unburied dead hangs heavily in the thick damp air. Their misshapened bodies are difficult to ignore. Some hang limp on the strands of barbed wire where they met death, while others lie partially submerged in the muck and muddy water. Swarms of feasting black flies rise from the dead, disturbed by our sudden appearance. We hurry to reach the airman.

We get to him before the Viets, thanks to the determined efforts of his friend. His guns are preventing the enemy soldiers from advancing any further. The injured pilot is an officer! He is excited to see us coming to his aid. He is unable to walk without extreme pain so we lend our support. Our weapons are not needed as the vigilant flyer overhead is witness to our rescue attempt. This pilot continues to master the communists with accurate deadly fire. They now realize that the capture of the pilot is improbable, so they begin to direct their fire at us. As the bullets zip through the air around us, several mortar rounds also explode nearby. But fortunately, and with great difficulty, we safely return through the minefields with the wounded officer.

As we tumble exhaustedly into a friendly trench, the officer cries out in extreme pain. A quick examination reveals a fractured right leg. Several volunteers carry the injured pilot to the field hospital on a litter of dirty canvas. His relieved comrade waves to us as he makes one last low pass over the trench before returning to the safety of his carrier.

CHAPTER 19

Not one has complained of Sergent Andersen's body odor for some time now. This is easily explained. We are surrounded by the unimaginable persistent stench of the irretrievable and unburied rotting bodies—both the enemies' and ours. Even though I remain hungry, I cannot eat if the wind is blowing in from the field of death. Hygiene and sanitation no longer exist. Water for drinking is severely rationed, and many good men have died on details attempting to bring some back from the river. Most drinking water is collected during the heavy rains. My USMC overalls have not yet begun to disintegrate in this wet climate. That cannot be said for other legionnaires. Their mud-stained uniforms are becoming more frayed and ragged every day.

*****

Poor Corporal Fulci. His malaria has returned, and there is little that we can do to make him comfortable. Although he claims to be freezing, his temperature is over 100 degrees. His teeth chatter constantly as he sits shivering under a moldy blanket in a corner of the dugout. He moans and occasionally calls out for his beloved Samira. We take turns looking in on him and providing him with whatever food or hot coffee that can be scavenged. He refuses the occasional sip of Vinogel, which we make by adding rain water to packets of dry wine crystals.

*****

The Day of Camerone has come and gone with very little cere-mony. Many of the legionnaires spoke loudly of "making Camerone" here in Dien Bien Phu. I was not one of them!

*****

The Viets are now using katyusha rockets, like the Russians in the Big War. The screaming rockets pound us for days without rest. Without adequate reinforcements and supplies, or a miracle of some kind, our defense will soon crumble. There is much talk of a possible breakout through the Viet lines—a surprise counterattack!

CHAPTER 20

I have concern for Sergent Andersen who has just been struck in the lower left leg by shell splinters. As Guenther and I carry him to field hospital, we pass a deep pit that has been dug by captured Viets. It is a nightmarish vision straight from hell itself. The pit is slowly being filled with dozens of human arms, legs, hands, and feet that have been amputated by the doctors in the adjacent hospital bunker. The discarded limbs have been sprinkled with a dusting of white lime, which makes the scene even more difficult to look upon.

Andersen's face, already grimacing from the pain of his wound, turns pale with shock upon seeing the gruesome pit. His eyes widen as he screams, "no! no! Don't let the butchers do that to me!" We try to console him, but Guenther and I both know that his leg is severely mangled, and it may, indeed, require removal if the old sergent is to live. Because of the unsanitary conditions and a limited supply of antiseptics, gangrene is presently the deadliest threat facing the surgeons.

Once our friend has been assured of treatment, we leave the underground chamber. I notice that women from the brothel are now assisting the hospital staff. I observe the women changing blood-soaked bandages, feeding warm soup to those who are unable to feed themselves, and supporting those who cannot stand or walk without help. I am warmed by these acts of comfort for the injured men. I know that the fate of many of these women was preordained by their culture and not of their own choosing. That does not seem fair to me.

*****

A captain from battalion headquarters makes his way through our trench. He carries a canvas satchel filled with decorations and promotions. I, myself, am surprised to find that I have been promoted from Soldier First Class to Corporal. I remember Vertov, the barber at Bel Abbes, and how he had predicted that, someday, I would achieve the rank of Legion Cabo. How many years ago had that been? Eight? Nine? The captain then surprises me further by pinning a ribbon to my mud-stained uniform. He says that I have been awarded a very high honor. The ribbon represents the Croix de Guerre. There is no ceremony, and no actual medal, but I am honored just the same. He explains that I have been awarded the medal, which I will receive later, for my actions in the rescue of the Navy pilot. Good friend, Vu, is also recognized with the presentation of a Colonial Army medallion for bravery. He smiles proudly when this is fastened to his shirt pocket. The captain has something for Sergent Andersen, but he is unable to find him. We explain that he has just been recently wounded and can be found at the hospital bunker. The captain leaves after presenting decorations to other weary, dispirited men.

*****

Under a moonless night sky, my detail of five men ventures out to booby trap the enemy trenches. When the Viet sappers return at first light with their picks and shovels, they will be greeted with our surprises. We return to our listening posts to wait for morning.

When morning comes, the ground is thick with white fog. As I sit alone in the listening post, which extends out fifteen or twenty meters from our main trench line, three white ghostly images slowly emerge from the fog and then cautiously move toward me. Their sudden appearance startles me. The white figures are no more than six meters in front of my position, and I have only seconds to respond. Taking careful aim, I fire my carbine until the magazine is empty. The three men are dead. They never realized that I was there. There is little doubt that all three are now dead. I freeze in my hole and wait nervously for more of the ghostly images to appear from the mist. It is to my great relief that none do. I leave the listening post to cautiously approach the three bodies. Each soldier is wrapped in a shroud of white parachute. This has rendered them practically invisible in the thick morning fog. I understand now how they were able to approach my position so easily without being seen. Each man is also carrying a pistol and two satchels filled with explosives. Still shaken by the event, I pause long enough to steady my nerves and calm a racing heart.

CHAPTER 21

Blackie and I, along with old Fulci, he, weakened by the return of the infernal malaria, carefully make our way to the medical bunkers to visit our friend, Sergent Andersen. It has been days since he received the injury to his leg, and we hope to raise his spirits with a taste of brandy. None of us are surprised by the vile conditions found in the growing maze of dugouts and trenches that have been appropriated for the wounded. Most of the men's wounds are noticeably covered with live maggots which are feeding on the dead tissue. I am already very aware of this practice. The overworked teams of doctors know that there is no alternative with the numbers of casualties mounting and the great demands on the insufficient supplies of antiseptics and penicillin. Many of the parachuted medical supplies land in the minefields where they cannot be recovered without risk, while others are lost when they are dropped into areas completely controlled by the Vietminh. We remain determined, however, to recover as much as possible.

With some difficulty, we are able to find our wretched-looking comrade lying on a bedroll in an open, unprotected trench. He is there with several other wounded men. Some appear to be recovering from their wounds, while others appear to be waiting for the relief that comes only with death. The injured men are crowded in the mire of the uncovered muddy trench floor. The orderlies and prostitutes are seen working together to assist those who are completely helpless. Others are left alone, abandoned to fend for themselves until conditions improve for everyone.

We are sad when we see that Sergent Andersen's leg has been amputated just below the left knee, but we all know that this procedure was necessary to save his very life.

He greets us with a weakened smile and then boasts defiantly, "They sawed my leg right off, and I watched them do it! And I know for certain they threw it in that pit just outside there!"

Blackie offers him the bottle of brandy, and he takes a cautionary first sip with obvious satisfaction. He seems to enjoy our company and welcomes the opportunity to talk. He continues on, but only after first bracing himself with another taste of brandy.

"Yes, they took my best leg, then gave me a medal. Why, hell, that captain gave everyone here a medal. Must have felt sorry for us?" He laughs and then speaks about the worsening conditions at the hospital. "I was trapped in that filthy bunker for two days. Couldn't breathe that disgusting air down there, so I created quite a loud disturbance, and they saw fit to move me up here, out in the open. I'd rather take my chances on getting shelled by the Viets out here than spend another minute breathing in that filth!" He pauses for a moment.

"Fulci! What in hell is wrong with you? You must look worse than I do!" Corporal Fulci, weakened by the walk here from the trenches, does not respond. Andersen turns to me. "Chapeau! My bandage has not been changed lately that I can remember. Go find a clean one for me. You are the only one in this lot I can trust to do a capable job of it, all right?" I nod and set out to find a suitable dressing, knowing that even the simplest items are in short supply.

Thirty minutes later, I return and change the dressing. During my absence, Sergent Andersen has had several more sips from the bottle of brandy and is even more talkative. "I have learned much while you were gone," he explains. "I understand that I have just had my bandage changed by a decorated hero…and a Cabo as well! That is wonderful news, Cabo Koob. I have enjoyed watching you grow into a man, and I am very proud of you! Now find me a crutch 'cause I'm going back to the trenches with you where I can do some good!"

The determined old sergent surprises everyone by rising effortlessly from the bedroll on his one sound leg and propping himself against a nearby supporting timber. Although each of us is amazed by the old legionnaire's grit, only Guenther questions Sergent Andersen's decision to return to the trenches in his weakened condition. Andersen replies, "You are right. I cannot walk to the trenches, even with a crutch. But you can carry me there because if I die here, without even a little fight, it will be a worthless death. At least, in the trenches, I will make the Viets pay dearly for my life! None of you can deny me that!" And no one does.

We quickly wrap Sergent Andersen's bedroll around two rifles, creating an improvised seat. Guenther, being the strongest, lifts the rear, while Blackie and I grab the front. Once Andersen is comfortably seated, the five of us begin to make our way back to our positions on the line. Two bandaged strangers, who have overheard Sergent Andersen's passionate request to die like a legionnaire, decide to join us. They follow behind at a short distance, struggling with each step in the sticky muck. If they make it to our position on the line, the remaining brandy will be waiting there for them.

CHAPTER 22

The katyusha rockets are not as frequent. Although that is significant for our morale, we sense that no miracle will happen here. We are now forced to use the last of our reserve ammunition while conditions worsen by the hour. Today, there are more rumors of a massive breakout that will include the entire battalion, cooks and all. I overhear that the regimental flag has already been cut up into small pieces, and these will be distributed among the NCOs for concealment. It would be a tremendous stain upon the battalion's proud history to have our colors captured and paraded by the Viets. As I am now a corporal, I am qualified to receive a section of the regimental flag for safeguarding. I make my way directly to the battalion command bunker to offer my services.

I am very fortunate as the captain responsible for the distribution of the flag is the same officer that appeared in our trench that day with his satchel of decorations. I am pleased to be remembered by the captain as he places a tightly rolled piece of the flag in my hand. I clutch it tightly, but once outside, I examine my piece more closely. Near the center of the rectangular strip of shiny white fabric are stitched the letters R A N. Each of the silk letters is bright gold and measures almost four fingers tall. I carefully roll the treasured cloth and then insert it into the bamboo section of my necklace. It, along with my keepsake bullet, will remain there for as long as necessary. My spirits have been greatly restored with this honor. I replace the wooden stopper and return to duty in the trench.

*****

The Viets are determined to overcome us in battle, for reasons I still do not understand. Whatever their cause, it will not fail as long as they continue to fight and die so bravely for it. We are most certainly in a predicament. Eight years...little comfort...very little gained. Until this very time, and maybe even, this very day, the Viets could feel the same as we concerning this merciless, unwinnable war. But now, they appear to have decisively won this fight, and maybe, the larger battle as well. I am still puzzled as to how the Viets were able to resupply their soldiers with heavy munitions and food enough for a siege that now continues beyond one hundred days.

CHAPTER 23

The order is given. Since victory will not be ours, and willful surrender has never been an option available to the Legion, a counterattack is wise. Most of us will either die or be captured, but a lucky few may get through in the confusion surrounding the breakout.

The seriously ill and wounded, which includes both Corporal Fulci and Sergent Andersen, will remain behind, along with a team of volunteers from the hospital staff to look after them. Their team also includes four willing women from the brothel who do not wish to be involved with the dangers of a breakout. No one can order them to leave since they are civilians. The crew of the last serviceable howitzer in the entire battery is also remaining at Isabelle. They have been ordered to fire a continuous barrage of smoke bombs to conceal those who will charge over the open ground into the jungle. Once they have exhausted their reserves of smoke bombs, the crew will sabotage the lone gun to keep the enemy from using it. They will then join the hospital staff in caring for the wounded.

Every able-bodied man in the garrison stands ready, nervously waiting to begin the charge through the Viet defenses and then, hopefully, on to freedom and fresh air. There will actually be two counterattacks to confuse the communists—one to the south, involving almost half of the battalion, and a second one to the east, with the remainder of the garrison.

I am separated from my company and comrades when the sergent-chef selects Vu and myself for a special assignment. I am disappointed in not being able to stand shoulder to shoulder with my close friends during this final attempt to escape, but the sergent's orders weigh heavier than any personal feelings. Before Vu and I leave the company to receive our instructions, I say farewell once again to my family—Guenther, Corporal Fulci, Blackie, and Sergent Andersen. I do not know when, or if, I will ever see them again. I wish them well.

The plan is simple. Legionnaires, carrying satchels filled with grenades, will advance through the smokescreen in front of each formation, throwing the explosives into the enemy-held trenches. They are to be followed closely by the rest of the garrison—first, those armed with the automatic weapons and then those with single-firing rifles. The sergent-chef informs me that Vu and I will not be in any of these groups during the counterattack. Instead, we have been ordered to escort a small party of civilians east toward the river, through the concealment of the smoke. It is thought to be our best chance for escape. The escape attempt will begin after the two offenses begin to the east and south.

A small group of civilians sit quietly, waiting for Vu and I to join them. In this group are three women and one man. The lone man is an elderly Chinese merchant, rumored to be of great wealth. Two of the women are from the Algerian brothel, while the other is a young Vietnamese woman with a calm presence. She is very beautiful. The faded green army coveralls that she wears are acceptable, however, I insist that the two prostitutes change from their colorful dresses into black coolie pants. This is quickly accomplished. Vu finds three discarded coolie bonnets and places one on the heads of the Chinese merchant and Algerian women.

Our supply of food is divided equally and then packed into two duffels, along with three wool blankets and two canvas tarps. The tarps can be joined together to create a rain shelter. This is all we will be allowed to take with us. Each bag is then fashioned to hang from the center of a sturdy bamboo pole. If we are seen by the Viets, I can only hope that they mistake the four civilians for Vietminh coolies. Vu, in his mud-splattered uniform, could easily be mistaken for a Viet soldier, but I can do nothing to conceal my size. I cannot consider shedding my own uniform when so many brave men will soon die in battle. Instead, I decide to wear a simple Viet bush hat, which I pull down tightly to conceal my Western features.

I am relieved that Vu will be with us since we have no map or compass. Our orders are very simple. We have been instructed to follow the river south until we have penetrated well beyond the areas controlled by the Vietminh. The river will eventually intersect with a larger river that flows west to east. I am told to follow this river east for approximately thirty kilometers where we should find a span of bridge still standing alongside an abandoned blockhouse. We are to wait there for others from the breakout while a recovery team is being dispatched to transport us out. As I said before, it is a simple plan.

The barrage of smoke bombs begins. There is barely enough time for a cup of weak coffee and a few spoonfuls of cold rations before the bugle sounds to signal the beginning of the main counter-attacks. The noise of the battle increases rapidly to our rear and south as we await the order to begin advancing toward the Nam Yum under the expanding smokescreen. The order does not come.

Meanwhile, neither advance is able to penetrate the Vietminh wall of bullets. Casualties mount as the stalled Legion forces realize they lack the numbers of men needed to successfully outflank the Viets' lethal machine guns. Just as the earlier orders to attack were simultaneous, so are the orders to withdraw. Both attacks are gallant, but each is doomed to fail. As the remaining survivors of the attacking main forces stagger back into Isabelle, a quiet order is given for our group to advance toward the river. It is now our time to try!

With Vu and I leading the four civilians disguised as Vietminh porters, we leave the firmer ground through the heavy smoke screen and proceed slowly through the muddy bog. This low-lying piece of ground is presently a swamp that has been created by the overflow from the rain-swollen river. Walking is difficult in the soft mire, but it is worth the extra effort because there are no minefields or trenches in our path to the river.

The heavy screen of smoke continues to hide our presence from the Viet sentries as we reach the east bank of the flooding river. After listening to the chaos of two hard-fought battles against their flanks, the enemy listening posts will be on extreme alert for any movement. Our greatest hope is to remain undetected in the smoke until we have passed well beyond the Viet forward positions. These are being manned by their best soldiers. If we are able to reach their inner ring of supporting troops and coolies, our disguises might be helpful.

With Vu leading cautiously out front, we continue following the east bank of the river. Each step now takes us a little further away from the protection of the smoke. The women and old man look convincing as porters as they shoulder the long bamboo poles between them in the customary manner. The Chinese merchant does not seem to mind being reduced to the lowly status of a coolie laborer. His partner in this deception is the older of the two women from the Arab brothel, while the other two women are paired together. I calculate that we have now walked at least 400 meters without being noticed. If our bit of luck holds until dark, it will be a miracle. Unfortunately, that miracle, if it does happen, will have been greatly enhanced by the diversion created by the garrison's failed counterattacks.

Suddenly, Vu signals for everyone to halt. A squad of Viet infantry has been spotted standing on a prominent sandbar about forty meters downriver from us. Either they have not seen us, or they are not overly concerned with our presence. Vu indicates that we will have to ford the river to the west bank immediately to avoid the soldiers. He leads the way. Once across the shallow waters, we take refuge in a small gully that is notched into the higher west bank. To our great comfort, the soldiers remain on the sandbar. Vu and I both notice that the gully leads away from the river for some distance. It is also deep enough to offer some concealment should we attempt to detour around the Viets on the sandbar. Since it will be dark soon, we settle ourselves onto the slippery banks of the gully to quietly wait for nightfall. I am concerned for my comrades and the battalion's attempted breakout an hour earlier.

While hiding in the ravine, we are startled to see hundreds of chattering Viet soldiers suddenly passing by us as they move upriver toward Isabelle. This can only mean one thing—another massive assault on the outpost. With their reserves of ammunition depleted, and now even more casualties as a result of the disastrous counterattacks, Isabelle cannot possibly withstand another assault. More enemy formations continue to advance by our hiding place. The unsuspecting soldiers walk so close to us that I can see their young, nervous but determined, faces in the failing light of the day. As expected, the big Viet guns now begin to ruthlessly pound the condemned camp. The shells whistle high over our heads just moments before they strike Isabelle with thunderous impact.

The orderly formations of Viet troops have finally passed by, but they are immediately followed upstream by hundreds of silent unarmed Vietnamese coolies. We must leave our hiding place now, at this exact moment, if we are to escape. With Vu still leading, we crouch down and continue slowly up the mud-slick gully about twenty meters. Here, it ends abruptly. Carefully raising my head to look out from here, I determine that we are still about forty meters from the cover of the jungle—and there is absolutely no concealment over that distance. Our ruse will have to work.

As we rise from the ravine, our heads are bowed to conceal our true identities. We move quickly, with the women and Chinaman shouldering the bamboo poles and packs containing our scant provisions. We cover the open distance to the forest without being detected, only to find that the jungle is alive with reserves of enemy soldiers and coolies. It is impossible to double back toward the river with so many of the enemy's forces directly in our path. We must continue further west, away from the river, if we hope to eventually outflank the widely dispersed rebels.

The artillery barrage of Isabelle has finally been lifted. This is a signal that the actual ground attack will begin very soon. I reach for the leather thong around my neck to ensure that it has not been lost.

We resume our detour west but occasionally venture south to determine the enemy's position. Each time, we are thwarted by the Viets' strong presence. We continue west for some distance, all this time, climbing a slight mountain whose forest has been scorched black in large areas by the napalm bombs. Perhaps this explains why there are no Viets on this part of the mountain. The heavy smell of ash and diesel fuel linger in the air. I encourage Vu to quicken his pace so that we can put this unpleasant place well behind us. The urgency to walk faster is readily understood by the civilians.

Nighttime comes, but we do not stop to sleep or rest since this is the best time to move without being discovered. Our pace remains incredibly slow and deliberate, but stealth is necessary if we are to avoid their lookouts. There is no more experienced man than Vu on this occasion. His keen instincts are responsible for our progress thus far.

Just before dawn, I signal for Vu to stop so that we may take food and rest. Everyone seems to be pleased with this decision although no words are exchanged. Tired looks befit each of us as we share several hard biscuits from the tinned rations, along with a few quick sips of warm canteen water. As the first light of morning begins to penetrate the jungle canopy, I find myself stricken again by the calm fascinating beauty of the young Vietnamese woman. She is no *congais*. Of that, I am certain.

My thoughts quickly return to the mission. Vu's natural sense of survival has been responsible for guiding us safely thus far through a wide, almost impenetrable, array of enemy forces, but we now find ourselves facing a greater problem! We are lost! There is little hope of ever finding the Nam Yum River, which is our way of finding the relief force. Meanwhile, the jungle has become a living hell. Our lone machete is ineffective in the attempt to penetrate the vines and undergrowth. These block us in every direction.

There are no animal paths or trails to be found, so Vu looks for streams or dry washes to follow whenever possible. The mountain streams and dry creek beds allow us to travel faster. We eagerly replace the fouled river water in our canteens with plenty of fresh, cool water from a small waterfall. This is the first unfouled water for any of us in over a month.

After struggling with the brutal conditions of the jungle for days, we discover that a high range of mountains is blocking our way to the south and further west. The mountains appear impassable. Vu indicates that we can only continue by going northwest. He points in that direction to an apparent distant gap between the high mountains. I continue to trust in his judgment.

Our few provisions will soon be exhausted, even with rations being reduced considerably more. Although wild game is plentiful in this area, as represented by the numerous sightings of small deer, monkeys and other varmints with furry tails, I fear that we might alert others to our presence if we fire our rifles. I decide that we will not hunt until we are too weak from hunger to continue. I am encouraged when no one objects. Perhaps, my companions are just too weak from hunger to dissent? I realize that I know nothing about them, not even their names.

The courageous nature of the civilians has been evident during this ordeal, however, the young Vietnamese beauty is, surprisingly, the most hardened of them! Never once have I seen fear or alarm in her perfect brown eyes, and I speak as one who has been distracted by them many times before.

CHAPTER 24

The jungle fights back! It does not wish to be invaded, and therefore, it challenges our every step. Small green leeches latch onto our bodies as we pass through the damp underbrush. These soon become round and plump from having their fill of our blood. Short lengths of split bamboo are used to scrape the leeches off, but others are always waiting to take their place. The seasonal rains are now raging, and the rain forest is abundant with slime-covered boulders. These slippery rocks are difficult to walk on, and each of us has fallen. Progress is better when we follow the streambeds, but unfortunately, these same streams are filled with black leeches. It is best to remove these before they have time to bite you, otherwise, the leech's small head will remain after its larger body has been scraped away. We work together to keep each other free of the unwelcome parasites. The banks of the creeks and streams are thick with growths of unavoidable thorn bushes. Their needle-sharp thorns tear at our clothes and bare skin. Bamboo vipers and other colorful snakes are abundant, but they usually slither away upon sensing our presence. This place is also home to nests of fierce hornets, blood-starved ticks, and mosquitoes as well as flesh-eating ants. Yesterday, we were startled by an encounter with a curious wild tiger and a spotted mountain lion. We safely avoid many dangers because of Vu.

*****

I must trust Vu, my loyal, dependable friend of eight years. The jungle frustrates him. He knows that this jungle will devour and swallow each of us if we remain too long. He works with little rest. Often, we encounter walls of impenetrable thorns. We then retreat in another direction, only to find that way blocked completely by a forest of giant bamboo or choking thickets of vines. Only hard truths await us in this environment. The jungle is discouraging, but we have little choice but to continue on. Our hopes lie in finding that low gap between the high mountains northwest of us. Perhaps, there is a river we can follow through the gap? Or perhaps, there is a trail or village? I must rely on Vu to lead us out before the remaining food is gone.

*****

We have been on this quest now for eight days, but we have exhausted only two days of rations. At the outset of our escape attempt, the Algerian women had contributed two small bags of dry weevil-free rice, a tin of sugar, and a pinch of sweet-smelling tea leaves. Likewise, I clearly recall the beautiful Vietnamese lady producing a single small bag of uncooked rice, two short sections of fresh sugar cane, and one lady's silk stocking, filled up to its ankle with small chunks of dried sweet potatoes. The sugar is good for restoring our energy, but it, like the rice and dried yams, is almost gone. Our current rations are barely enough to support one man for four days; instead, these rations must sustain six active hungry adults indefinitely.

We stop to camp for the night near a fast-flowing stream with several waterfalls. The three women step off quickly to the nearest waterfall to wash themselves and their tattered clothing in the icy mountain water. They can be heard laughing softly as they splash about. One can be heard humming a cheerful tune. We take off our packs, belts, and rifles and hurry with the Chinaman to join them, but the humming stops just before we arrive. After a good wash and a careful check for leeches, I build a small fire to warm us while our clothing dries. The fire is appreciated in the cold evening air. Everyone gathers around its warmth, being careful to allow extra space for the kneeling merchant.

He is busy boiling an exact measure of rice. After it is cooked, he forms the sticky rice into six balls of equal size. We each take one, aware that the rice ball and a thimble-sized chunk of dried sweet potato must last until camp is prepared tomorrow. Before the campfire is completely extinguished for the night, a few tea leaves are added to a canteen cup half-filled with hot fresh water. As the cup of tea is being passed around, I wonder if my fellow legionnaires are safe tonight and if they are blessed with any food at all?

*****

We are surely the only humans to have ever willingly ventured into this forbidden hell. This is a troubling thought. I must continue to trust in Vu's guidance if I am to return this party to French territory. I believe that we have now crossed the border into Laos, but that is of little concern. Two of our original packs are discarded in the jungle after they are emptied of the last remaining rations; however, we retain the one duffel that still contains the blankets and pieces of canvas. Hunger is now an issue of grave importance. We must have fresh game if we are to have the strength to fight our way out of this predicament.

We are now forced to eat only what the jungle provides for us. Our first hunting party is successful as I am able to kill a large python with a single bullet. The roasted snake meat is sweet and very good, but painful stomach cramps follow soon for those who have eaten too much. The surplus meat is allowed to dry slowly over the dying campfire coals. It will sustain us well tomorrow.

CHAPTER 25

Every step through this green prison brings us closer to the higher range of mountains. We are greatly encouraged after sighting the low gap, estimated to be no more than two or three days' distance from where we now stand. With spirits renewed, we follow closely behind Vu. His smile has returned. At the end of another hard-fought day of battle with the briars and thorn bushes, we make camp and perform the now-routine inspections for hidden leeches, ticks, and white lice. Afterward, we eat our only food for the day—several bites of dried snake meat with the last few sips of weak tea. Tomorrow, we must find food or succumb to the jungle.

The noise of the heavy morning rain conceals our presence as we stumble clumsily through the wet underbrush. Luckily, Vu has happened upon a large unsuspecting turtle, which he quickly bashes on the head with his rifle butt. He places the dead turtle in the duffel. Later, when we stop for the day, it will be cooked, if enough dry wood can be found. If not, then we will have no choice but to eat the turtle meat raw. Only six matches remain. These must certainly be used wisely. I remain hopeful of finding other game to go with the turtle as we move closer to that gap at the base of the high mountains.

We have no further luck hunting, but we are another day closer to our objective. We halt to make camp just before dark. Fortunately, enough dry wood is collected for a fire. Vu wanders off into the nearby underbrush and soon returns with a handful of freshly dug roots. He smiles proudly as he holds out the sweet-smelling roots for everyone to see. Then he removes the cooking pot and turtle from the duffel, fills the pot halfway with water, and places it in the fire. Using his knife, he removes the large shell from the turtle and then places the carcass in the pot of slowly heating water. Next, he takes six giant acorns from his jacket pocket. We look on curiously as the huge nuts are cracked, removed from their shells, and tossed into the pot with the turtle. The thin layer of bark is then stripped from the handful of sweet roots, and these roots are also added to the pot. The strange mixture is soon stewing briskly over the hot coals as we look on, hungrily awaiting our first and only food for this day.

When Vu is satisfied that all is ready, he pours the hot liquid from the pot into the canteen cup, filling it. The cup with the clear broth is then carefully passed around to our anxious waiting hands, and everyone takes their fair share. I can feel my energy slowly returning. Vu then gives each of us one of the large acorns. These are very, very bitter, but my stomach does not object. Next, he skillfully cuts the warm turtle carcass into six pieces and gives each of us a share. I savagely attack my piece. After this is gone, Vu encourages everyone to chew on the bittersweet roots that rest in the bottom of the cooking pot. These quickly disappear as well.

The mountain man has even saved the bark that was stripped from the sweet roots. These are boiled up in a canteen cup of water to create a clear tea. It is significant to note that no one reacts unfavorably to the odd but satisfying meal. The little montagnard has saved us for now, but I am uneasy because there is no food left for tomorrow. My faith in Vu remains strong.

*****

The two Algerian women have become good friends. They can now be heard talking softly to each other in Arabic, which no one else understands. The beautiful Vietnamese woman occasionally speaks with the old Chinaman in Vietnamese which, again, no one else understands. Vu and I are alone in that no one is likely to understand anything that either of us would say. It is truly amazing to find that six individuals from five different countries have been able to survive and exist in these conditions for this long without speaking. I have grown tired of my own silence. It is extremely possible that the young woman, like so many others in her country, has been schooled in French, but I will never know unless I ask. Vu speaks when he chooses to, always repeating the same statement. "Cabo Dieter! You same children, children same you!" It never changes.

We break camp before daybreak to cover as much ground as possible. After all of our efforts, the high mountains still seem so far away. By midday, we have become exhausted, but no one objects to the decision to continue on. As we move on, we stumble blindly onto a well-used animal track. Vu thinks the track might lead to a watering hole, which is the best place to look for fresh game. After the civilians are instructed to rest until we return, Vu and I follow the track. He is right! It leads directly to the waters of a nearby stream. On the nearest sloping bank, there are the obvious signs of recent visits here by animals of differing sizes. We move downstream a short distance and wait, hidden behind a thicket of thorn bushes. Our wait is very short. We have just barely made ourselves ready when a tiny deer bounces quietly onto the sandy bank and begins to sniff cautiously at the air and footprints of the previous visitors to the creek. Satisfied that the sand bar is safe, the small deer lowers its head for a drink from the stream. I take very careful aim and fire once. The little deer jumps high in the air and then collapses onto the sandbar, lifeless. I am very proud of my marksmanship because the little deer was such a challenging target. We hurriedly leave our blind to claim our grateful prize. Our hunting is over anyway, since the rifle shot is sure to have frightened off any other approaching game.

Vu laughs as he examines the kill. He cannot find any marks on the tiny deer, and neither can I. It seems that I did not shoot the deer after all. The timid creature must have simply died from fright when startled by the unexpected loud noise of my rifle shot. Nonetheless, we quickly dress the animal on the narrow sand bar and return to the others with our good fortune. The spirits of the camp are renewed by the sight of fresh game.

As we sit near the warmth of the dying cookfire coals, I look at each of those of our party. I have been ordered to escort them to safety, so there can be no peace for me until this has been done. Tonight, we have food. Tomorrow, we will be stronger.

The Vietnamese woman, who has been talking quietly with the Chinaman, moves over to sit beside me. She smiles and asks if I understand French. I nod yes. She says the Chinaman has told her that we are now in Laos, and have been for over a week. The Chinaman also believes that if we continue on our same course that we will eventually reach China. He knows of a large trading town across the border in China, but we cannot go there because of armed bandits who always kill their victims. She says the Chinaman is nervous because he carries many gold coins in a leather pouch hidden underneath his waistband. The Chinaman believes this money might eventually be used to purchase food or other provisions once we find a friendly hamlet. His name is Lin Yang. She points to the older of the two Algerian women. "She is Douda. Her friend is named Zora." Lin Yang, the Chinese merchant, knows well the usefulness of gold.

I thank her for sharing this information and ask for her name. She responds by removing a folded piece of yellow paper from her shirt pocket. The paper is a Vietnamese Army document that identifies her as Mrs. Hanh Long, wife of Captain Vinh Long, an officer in the First Vietnamese Parachute Battalion. The identification paper says that she is married! This is difficult news for Legionnaire #494321. She is married!

As I return the paper to her hand, she asks, "What is your name?"

I respond, "My name is Dieter Koob. My Laotian friend is Vu."

She asks, "Are you German?"

I answer, "Yes! Berlin was my home."

She listens and then tells how she was allowed to join her husband at Dien Bien Phu in January but became stranded there in the deteriorating conditions. Her unfortunate situation worsened even greater three weeks later when the captain was killed while leading his men in a counterattack against the Vietminh. Friends of her husband took care of her until the conditions at their outpost became even more disastrous. She was then secreted to Isabelle where the possibility of an escape seemed to be greater. And now she sits here at my campfire. Mrs. Hanh Long, a strong, brave woman who deserves better than this.

CHAPTER 26

Morning! And after a half day of battle with the stubborn underbrush, there is, at last, a true reason to be happy. We have temporarily escaped from the confines of our jungle prison! Now we cautiously emerge from the shaded canopy of thick hardwoods onto an enormous flat plain of sunny grassland. We shield our weakened light-starved eyes as they adjust to the brilliance of the midday sun. The sweet welcome smell of drying grass replaces that of the decaying jungle. A closer inspection of my tired, weary party reveals many deep scratches, cuts, sores, and inflamed insect bites, but we are healthy otherwise. From here, the draw between the mountains appears to be one day's journey, just far enough to exhaust our current supply of water and dried venison. It is my decision to cut the water ration in half since our next water source is unknown. We tromp off through the tall grass with hopes of finding a passageway through the mountain range ahead.

*****

The afternoon's march covered much ground, but it is now clear that we will not reach the pass before dark. It is very close, however. We stop to camp for the night in an area of waist-high grass that is flattened down with a piece of the canvas. The evening is warm, and an old familiar sky is seen for the first time in weeks. The evening sky is charged with menacing dark gray clouds that pass swiftly overhead. The second canvas tarp is kept near in case a heavy rain should catch us out in the open. There will be no fire tonight.

Vu wakes me in the middle of the night. It is my turn to stand guard. Stirring is difficult because I had been sleeping so restfully on the soft thick cushion of grass. Everyone sleeps soundly as I slowly rise. We have been spared from any rain during the night, but deep thunder bellows from a distant lightning-filled sky. Something else reaches our camp as well—the distinct smell of wood smoke! Someone is very near!

I quickly wake Vu and inform him of my discovery. We both agree that the winds are carrying the smoke from a distant area in the general direction our party is headed. And there is too little smoke for it to be coming from a wildfire. We have no choice. Vu and I, under cover of the cloudy moonless night, must leave now to find the source of the smoke.

I wake Hanh. My instructions to her are simple. "Everyone must wait here until we return!" She understands. We set out immediately, aware that our return to the camp will be easy to retrace through the trampled grasses.

The smell of wood smoke grows stronger as we continue on. Soon, an open campfire can be seen clearly through the thinning grasses. Three armed men surround the roaring fire. There is also a thatched dwelling on stilts in the center of a small clearing. The light from a fuel lantern shines brightly through the open door and windows. The house appears to be unoccupied and in need of much repair. Whoever these men are, they must feel secure with their open fires and bright lanterns here this night. They seem to have little use for caution and behave as if they have full command of their surroundings.

Vu's interest in the men has now grown stronger. He quietly slips closer to overhear their words. When he returns an hour later, Vu strongly opposes having any contact with these men. They must be avoided. That is all I need to know! We quickly make our way back to camp to find everyone waiting for our return. After the party is warned of the presence of armed men, we leave our camp, taking a longer route to the edge of the northern grasslands. This detour sufficiently flanks around the armed men in the clearing.

Our excellent progress through the grass flats allows us to reach a forest of hardwoods rooted at the base of the high mountain range. We rest briefly in the cool shade and then continue on toward the mountain draw where a passageway or trail might most likely be located. Unless they have left the clearing, the armed men are far to the south and now represent no threat to us. Our spirits are lifted when we discover a narrow, but well-used foot trail coming from the direction of the house in the clearing. It is our hope that this trail will lead us to other people, or maybe even a village where food can be found. With Vu leading far ahead at a considerable distance, we set out again in a single file.

The footpath stretches further into the breach between the mountains and, soon, merges with a small swift-flowing river. The old trail, which now follows the river through a deep winding valley, climbs gradually up into the hilly hardwoods. Tall craggy peaks of white limestone rise above the canopy of treetops on both sides of the valley. The steep pillars of rock are completely barren except for the presence of some stubborn climbing vines and creepers. It is a good, easy trail to follow, having been maintained over time by those who have been dependent upon it. Regardless of the trail's condition, we are tired, weary from hunger, and must rest very soon. We have not eaten today.

Vu waits ahead on the trail. He has news! I learn that our montagnard scout has discovered a small hamlet of five dwellings ahead. The settlement sits in a clearing on the trail near the river. He reports seeing at least two men with long rifles and three women tending a field of corn. One of the men wore the helmet of the Vietminh. He saw no old people or children or animals. Vu thinks that it will be better if we wait until nightfall and then follow the river around the village until it rejoins the trail. We are tired and weak, and there is likely to be food here, but I must trust Vu since he has guided us safely through a trackless jungle. Vu is correct! The village openly harbors the Vietminh, and it must be avoided. Upon being made aware of the situation, the hungry Chinaman with the gold coins remains silent. He, too, has learned to value Vu's judgment.

It is decided. After night falls, we purposely avoid the trail and the village by wading upstream in the river. To our surprise and great delight, the field of young corn does not appear to be guarded. While we watch from the river's edge, the women crouch low as they sneak into the field to pluck several ears from the stalks. They are careful to leave no telltale signs of their poaching. The women then brush away their footprints as they back quietly out of the field to rejoin us in the river. After a short distance, the trail is easily located again. Once we have traveled a safe distance from the settlement, we move off the trail to rest for the night and feast on an ear of sweet ripe com.

In the morning, we continue upward into the mountains at a strong pace. Vu, who was born into a mountain existence, is the only one whose stamina is not being challenged by the thin air of this extreme altitude. We climb higher, and when our pace slows, he urgently encourages us to continue pressing onward.

The river, which has been gradually fed by many smaller connecting creeks and streams, is now reduced to a narrow stream. After many hours of difficult climbing, we take the opportunity to rest and refill our canteens at a point where the narrowing trail suddenly veers sharply away from the stream. Vu does not seem concerned that the trail and stream have now separated. He urges us on even more. From this altitude, our exhausted bodies are humbled by a magnificent view of surrounding mountains. We rest briefly and then continue to climb!

Our trail ends abruptly in a small canyon with high walls. Is it possible that this trail of two days has led us nowhere? We sit to rest but watch in amazement as Vu disappears by squeezing his body through a small fracture in the rock face. He soon returns and encourages us to stand and follow him back through the narrow opening. He has found a smaller footpath which, unlike the other trail, goes straight up the mountainside. This difficult trail also seems to end soon, but Vu is undaunted. With little difficulty, he discovers yet another hidden path that also continues straight up for a short distance and then stops abruptly. Again Vu is able to find another well-hidden path. Several times during the climb, the trail apparently ends, only to be found again by Vu. He seems to have the uncanny ability to pick it up again—almost as if he has been here before.

As we reach higher into the thinning air, breathing becomes even more difficult for everyone. Vu continues to encourage us to keep moving. Several times, we encounter other less difficult trails crossing our own, but Vu always insists that we stay on the steepest climb. I must rely on the excited little man. His actions seem to indicate that better things lie ahead. We continue.

Camp for the night is made beside the path, and the last of the com is eaten. I use the last match to build a small fire for warmth after Vu assures me that it will be safe to do so.

The matches have given us much comfort, and without them, our circumstances will become ever more difficult. Everyone is soon asleep, exhausted by the strenuous climb and the insufficient nature of the air at this altitude.

CHAPTER 27

I wake first in the morning and discover that Vu is missing. Shortly after I notify the others of his absence, Vu suddenly appears on the trail ahead of us. He is not alone! With him are four dark-skinned men, armed with old rifles and machetes, wearing the clothing and head wrappings that are typical of the Laotian montagnards I had seen in the Tonkin. It is too late to reach for my rifle. As the men come closer, I notice that Vu does not appear to be their prisoner, in fact, he is still carrying his rifle.

The strange men approach to get a better look at our surprised faces. Vu smiles and then says something which makes the other men laugh. One of the men removes a sack from his shoulder and hands it to Douda. At first, she is reluctant to take it. Vu encourages her, indicating that something pleasant is in the bag. The other men laugh at Vu's words. She opens the bag and takes out several raw yams and a large piece of roasted meat. It is food! They have brought us food! Soon, we are eating and wondering who are these men with Vu, and why are they befriending us? The men cautiously walk over to where I am standing. They seem to be extremely interested in me for some unknown reason, showing little concern for the women and Chinese merchant. Perhaps they have never seen a European before today? Vu joins the men as they circle around me for a closer inspection. He speaks to them as he points to me, and they each smile and nod their heads in agreement with what he has just said. I am confused about why I am receiving this much attention from these strange men.

After we have eaten our fill, Vu indicates that we must continue further on up the trail with him and the other men. We follow after them, our bodies now encouraged by the unexpected food. The trail takes us even higher, until we reach the very summit of the highest mountain. From here, I am startled to see a complete village nestled below in a great basin. The primitive village appears to be surrounded on all sides by high cliffs.

The sound of drums can be faintly heard in the distance. The drumming becomes louder now as it echoes outward from the settlement below. As we descend down the trail toward the village, we encounter several sentries with rifles. I assume the guards are there to protect the village from those who are unwelcome. The sentries eye us curiously as we pass, making no effort to stop us. I sense that they already knew that we would be arriving. Our escort halts after leading us into the heart of the village, where a throng of very interested villagers slowly surround us. They move forward to eye us better. Others wander out from their dwellings and gardens to join the gathering.

I see many things. The houses of this village do not stand on stilts. Each is constructed with walls of split bamboo and roofs of thatched palm leaves. A small stable for animals sits beside each house. Some of the stables are empty, while others contain pigs and oxen. Many chickens roam freely. A pack of skinny barking dogs have now joined the villagers. The dark-skinned people talk and gesture excitedly among themselves as they look us over in amazement. We are just as amazed by them. Our sudden presence here in their village seems to be cause for great alarm.

The broad-smiling Vu is no stranger here as many of the villagers greet him openly with enormous smiles of their own. He takes my hand and quickly leads me into the swelling crowd, stopping suddenly before a large collection of children.

He calls out loudly, "Tong! Neng!"

To my great astonishment, two shy young boys cautiously emerge from the crowd. I am amazed to discover that each of the boys has blue eyes and golden yellow hair—as my own! Their light, fair skin is completely unlike that of those around them. It is an unbelievable sight! The two boys look very unnatural and out of place among the dark children gathered around them. Vu gives each of the boys a big hug and then turns to look at me.

He says, as he has said many times before, "You same children, children same you!" He pushes the older of the two before me and says, "Tong." He grabs the arm of the smaller child and says, "Neng." I am very confused! These two boys are truly Vu's children! I have looked into his ever-smiling face now for many years, and it is plainly obvious to me that the boys share the same smile as their father. But where is the mother, the wife? Vu reaches into the crowd and takes the hand of a happy young woman. She is the wife he left behind when he became an army scout. He offers the woman's name as "Lo" as he stands proudly beside her and the two unusual sons. Lo's skin is very dark, and the hair underneath her turban appears dark and silky. I find it difficult to accept that she is the birth mother of Vu's sons.

It seems that Vu has intentionally guided us to this particular village. It is his village! I am certain of this, and only he knows the true reason for doing so. I do know that we would have perished in the jungle long before today if not for his help. He has safely delivered us to this village, and for that, I am grateful.

The women, Zora, Douda, Hanh, and Lin Yang, the merchant, have been led to a large building in the center of the village. This longhouse sits on a rise of land which overlooks the village. I join them with Vu, his wife, and sons. As we stand before the great house, wondering what might happen next, a sudden silence comes over the villagers. Even the children become quiet as they seek out their own families. Two men emerge from the longhouse and slowly approach us. They seem greatly alarmed by our presence. One of the men is decorated around his neck with many shiny bands of silver coins. The second man displays no silver jewelry but wears a turban filled with brightly colored feathers. A cape of striped tiger skin rests over his shoulders. His dark nervous eyes look us over in a haunting manner. These men must be very important in this village. They speak in whispers to each other, while the curious villagers continue to remain perfectly silent. I wonder if the silence is offered out of respect or fear—or possibly both! The two men stop directly before us.

Vu is summoned to come forward by the man wearing the silver necklaces. He must be the village leader. The little scout joins the two men as they continue patiently examining each of us. The turbaned man questions Vu. I believe he asks Vu to explain why he has brought five strangers to their village. Vu is obviously uncomfortable in their presence, but his answer seems to please them.

We are each asked to stand apart from the others of our group. Vu continues to answer their questions as we are individually identified, studied, and discussed by the two inquisitive men. I am identified first as the leader. There is much discussion between the two regarding my physical features from the neck up. Mister Yang, the Chinese merchant, draws little attention from the examining men, as do Douda and Hanh, but the leader seems to be especially interested in Zora. The exotic beauty is not concerned with the attention being given to her by this stranger. Seven weeks ago, in the camp brothel, it was the only life she had.

Vu continues to answer their questions. The chieftain leader then addresses the quiet watchful villagers. Once released from their conditioned silence, they respond with an outburst of noisy chatter. Many men approach Vu to welcome him home. They are happy because Vu has returned safely from France's war with the Vietminh. They are also happy because the village chief has just declared that tomorrow will be a day of great celebration to thank the good spirits for Vu's safe return. Everyone is happy!

After a restful night in the lodge of Vu's family and clan, I am awakened by the commanding voice of the man with the haunting eyes. Vu explains that this man is the village sorcerer and provider of all medicine. The medicine man indicates that I am now forbidden to leave the Lolo village—this startling message being a personal order from the village chieftain. The sorcerer, whose name is Dok, also warns that, even though escape is impossible, any attempts at such foolishness would enrage the chieftain. I am made aware that, I, like Vu's unusually fair-skinned sons, am perceived to be a gift to the entire village from the spirits of their benevolent ancestors. Vu seems sorrowful upon hearing the chieftain's decree, after all, it was he who brought me here. He never assumed that his chieftain would rob me of my freedom. Regrettably, I also realize that Vu is powerless to help me. The tribal chieftain has absolute authority and must always be obeyed. His words have condemned me. I am now prisoner here.

CHAPTER 28

By my very best calculations, I determine that six months have passed. This village is so isolated from the rest of the world that its existence seems more mythical than real. Much has happened, but I still remain a prisoner. The village's opium harvest several months ago was followed soon afterward by the arrival of a small expected party of Chinese drug merchants. Guards had been sent down the mountain trail to meet them and guide them back to the village. During their brief visit, Lin Yang, my former Chinese ward, bargained with his sizable sum of gold for passage to a settlement rumored to be somewhere on the Big River twenty miles west of here. His coins also purchased passage for the beautiful Hanh Long and Douda, who lately had become increasingly more appealing to the eyes of Mister Yang, the Chinaman. It was best for them to leave here as soon as possible because the Lolos despise all outsiders. However, the villagers do manage to hide their contempt of the Chinese opium merchants because they always bring with them many crates filled with equal weights of salt and silver coins.

Before Hanh left the village, I wished her a safe journey, knowing that we would never see each other again. I had failed in my mission to escort the four civilians back to French territory, but there was still some hope for her yet. She hopes to be reunited with her father and relatives eventually in Saigon City in the south. She vowed to report my circumstances to French authorities whenever possible. My heart was heavy as I witnessed their departure. I grieve also for my friends—Blackie, Gunther, Corporal Fulci, and Sergent Andersen. I will never know their fate as long as I remain stranded at the top of the world.

CHAPTER 29

Three years have passed! During this time, the soils of the main poppy field and vegetable gardens were exhausted of all mineral value and had to be abandoned—along with the entire village. A site for the new village was selected at a considerable distance from the old one, and work was begun at once on clearing new fields for planting. The tribesmen started large controllable fires that filled the sky with thick smoke. After several days of burning, the fires had consumed all the trees and brush in the area to be planted. No effort was made later to remove the numerous tree trunks scattered throughout the new ashen fields even though this would have been an easy task for a team of strong oxen.

The new village was constructed while the fields were being readied for planting. I discovered that frequent moving is a common practice of the Lolos and other tribes that depend on their gardens for survival. As is their custom, the communal long house, with its steep roof of thatched leaves, was constructed in the exact center of the new village. A nearby stream provides a plentiful source of fresh water.

It is peaceful here. I do not miss the misery of war. Although I am forbidden to venture away from the village unless an armed tribesman is with me, I have been accepted by the superstitious Lolos. Vu remains my faithful ally. His clan graciously provides for all my needs of shelter, food, and clothes. In return, I labor in the family's garden of beans, corn, cabbage, melons, and other strange unrecognizable vegetables. At the end of each day, when the poppy fields and plants have been tended to, the dust-covered tribesmen in their tight-fitting skullcaps pass their clay jars containing a brew made of fermented rice. It is quite pleasant tasting, but the alcohol in it kicks like a bee-stung mule.

The women are happy. They wear silver jewelry and colorful dresses with red aprons and silver buckles. Their long dark silken hair is customarily wrapped in turbans of dark cloth. It was the women of the village who first introduced me to the pleasures of the opium pipe. I quickly learned that opium provided me with an imaginary escape from my actual prison. In this opium-created dreamworld, my freedom no longer has value. Escape no longer matters. Lost friends no longer concern me. I lose spirit with the taking of each pipe. There is no truth, hard or soft, when the brain is percolated by opium.

Vu still remains sorrowful in my presence, even though I have declared him to be innocent of any wrong. I was always certain that each step we took through the jungle was the right step. I continue to believe that. However, my attempts to ease his guilt prove fruitless. His sons, Tong and Neng, are rapidly growing and enjoy being in my company. When together, the three of us present an unusual sight for the other Lolos. I am not a good student, and the young boys struggle to make even the simplest words of their language known to me. Lo, their watchful mother, is pleased to see them playing with me, and I am pleased to act like a child for the first time in my life. I have adopted a puppy, and I have named him Tony. That was the name of Tom Mix's horse. I have taken no permanent companion or mistress even though there are many gentle-featured maidens here among the villagers. Each of them is skilled in the preparation and offering of the opium pipe.

The many frequent celebrations and noisy festivals promoted by Tan, the chieftain, serve to break the tranquility of routine village life. Most celebrations begin with the sacrifice of a squealing pig or ox. Drinking the warm blood of the sacrificed beast is necessary to please the good spirits of deceased ancestors. These are the good phi. They keep the fierce phi away from the village in the deepest jungle where they can do little harm. Likewise, the silver jewelry and shiny objects worn by the villagers are also considered to be effective for confusing the evil spirits. These evil phi can bring great harm and discord to the entire village if they get too close. Only Dok has the uncanny ability to sense their presence. If the sorcerer feels that the fierce phi are near, he immediately orders loud drumming to begin as well as the continuous banging of a large metal gong in front of the longhouse.

There is much to eat and drink on the days of celebration. Many clay jars, once filled with rice wine, lie scattered about. The villagers feast on odd things like bat wings, boiled tree bark, pig feet, and frogs. I enjoy the buffalo steaks after they have been roasted over a hot fire. The last celebration continued for three days and nights. This festival was to celebrate Tan's taking of Zora as his wife. The exotic Algerian beauty seemed fated to capture the heart of the powerful chieftain.

Tan is a fair man. He rewards us for our labors in the poppy fields with a choice of one silver coin or an equal weight of salt. Although salt is very precious, I always choose a coin because its worth might serve me later.

Dok views me with suspicion. His interest in me increased greatly when he learned from Vu that I possessed powers to aid the sick and injured. Vu was most likely referring to my duties as a medical orderly. This has presented a great dilemma for the sorcerer because he now feels threatened by my presence. Dok would never allow another man to do medicine in his village. He believes that his power over the minds and bodies of the villagers can never be shared. He will share his vast wisdom with no one, for that would weaken his great power. But since he has openly proclaimed me to be a gift from the good phi, he is reluctant to petition the chieftain for my expulsion from the village.

CHAPTER 30

Thirteen years have passed since the beautiful Vietnamese lady, Hanh, left the village with Douda and the Chinamen. This I have determined to be correct because I have been rewarded with exactly twenty-six silver coins for my labors in the poppy fields—a coin from each of the two yearly harvests. I am a wealthy subject of the chieftain, and my health is still good.

Much has happened in the ten years since the marriage of Tan and Zora Dwing. At this time, the entire village was moved twice to new locations with better soil, each site being personally selected by the sorcerer. Vu's two sons, Tong and Neng, are grown and have each taken a wife. Tong's wife has given birth to a son, who has dark features like all the other children in the village. Zora has also given birth to three children. She is a good mother and happy to have escaped the despair of life in the brothel. I have taken no mate as the opium pipe remains my true mistress. I have learned the words of the Lolos and many of their customs. On two occasions, I have also helped defend the village from marauding strangers. Those mongrels will never return!

Shiny silver airplanes fly high in the skies overhead. The mysterious planes are unlike any that I have ever seen before. Their pilots do not seem interested in our village as they streak by. We are grateful that the bombs they carry are not intended for us. Vu believes that the strange planes are still hunting for the Vietminh, but the sorcerer insists the planes are filled with the evil phi. He warns that they will soon be strong enough to challenge his powers and then there will be much suffering. No one dares to question his judgment.

In the week that follows, many of the villagers, including the chieftain, become stricken with painful stomach cramps. Those affected by the mysterious illness display uniform signs of high fever, weak pulse, chills, diarrhea, nausea, vomiting, and the painful stomach cramps. Because the ill are unable to keep down food or water, their conditions worsen. Several members of the tribe die in agony from the severe dehydration brought on by this cursed disease. At first, I thought that those who were stricken ill had merely eaten poisoned food, but I now believe the village water supply has been contaminated with germs. When I inform Dok that the water has most likely been poisoned by the bad phi, he commands everyone to stop drinking from the stream. Water for the village must now be brought from a source in the next valley. It will be a major task to transport enough water to meet the village needs, but it must be done.

Dok also gives orders for the clan houses of deceased victims to be burned to keep the evil spirits at bay. He also commands that the drumming and beating of the gong continue until the conditions in the village improve. His orders are followed, but this has no effect as others soon fall victim. More houses are burned. The affected grow so weak that they cannot speak above a whisper while their bodies shiver frantically to stay warm. The sorcerer, realizing that he must attend to the needs of Tan before anyone else in the village, enlists my aid. I will do whatever I can to help!

I examine the chieftain. He winces in pain to the lightest touch of his stomach. His wrinkled rapidly dehydrating body will not accept even a simple taste of water. If he continues to lose his battle to retain some water, he will die like the others. I share my thoughts with Dok, and he immediately prepares a warm tea. The tea contains fresh water, tree moss, lichens, and sugar. In an effort to raise the chieftain's body temperature, his cool shivering body is rubbed with a liniment made from a mixture of animal grease and ground hot peppers. Some of the villagers are rubbing the sick bodies with warm ashes from the fires. This treatment works to reduce the shivering as effectively as the hot liniment.

To our great surprise, Tan is suddenly able to retain the weak tea when taken in small sips. This continues over a period of many hours. This is the first good sign. A mixture of rice gruel and powdered opium are given to the ailing chieftain in hopes of relieving the painful bowel discomfort, and in less than twenty-four hours, the pain there subsides considerably. Still, he is too weak to lift his arms. Dok shares this information with the other villagers, and they set about, hurriedly preparing the tea and gruel mixtures for the sick. There is a measure of relief and hope now in the village, but this battle is far from being won. Those who are now able to ingest small amounts of liquid and gruel for the extreme abdominal pain are still weak from extended dehydration and feeble pulse. I tell Dok that we must give Tan's body enough strength to fight the bad spirits which have entered his body. Dok listens and decides that another brew of tea will be made from ground mustard seeds and dark raw opium. At first, we are worried when Tan's body refuses this powerful tonic, but our hopes rise when he is finally able to accept the liquid. Soon afterward, I observe a slightly stronger pulse in the chieftain. This is good news, which I readily share with Dok. After all, it was his idea to stimulate Tan's body with the potent brew. The chieftain is very weak and unable to speak, but he does respond with a smile—his first in many days! Zora, who has remained at her husband's side since he first became stricken, now leaves to share the news with others.

A few houses have escaped the fires that were set intentionally to frighten away the evil phi. These dwellings continue to provide shelter for the sick. The drumming continues as ordered by Dok—but so does the dying. I estimate that one-fourth of the villagers are now affected by this mysterious plague, and if our judgment is wrong, many of the living will join the dead. Even with all of our efforts, we were unable to save Lo. Vu and his sons prepare her for burial. I cannot explain why some of us have not been stricken? Is there a reason for our good fortune? A purpose? Perhaps there is a truth yet to be uncovered? I am suddenly filled with memories of my sister for the first time in years. I realize that too many of those years have been lost to the opium pipe.

*****

The dying stops. There is neither a means nor a process here that can determine if our efforts helped in the recovery from the epidemic. It would be helpful to know in the event a similar dread strikes the village again.

A week has passed, and Tan has declared that a festival will take place to celebrate the victory over the villainous phi. Ancestors and the recently deceased victims of the phi's scourge on the village will also be honored during this celebration. They are to be remembered as warriors who gave their lives in the village's great battle against their constant enemy—the evil phi.

CHAPTER 31

Tan has stunning news for me! He is convinced that Dok and I saved his life as well as the lives of many villagers. At the festival, he will officially grant my freedom and provide me with two escorts to the settlement on the Big River. I am filled with great uncertainty. I struggle to think of a life away from this mountain. I remember the names of my dearest friends from another time, remembered because I promised never to forget them. I know nothing of the world outside. I have become a member of this tribe in every respect. I have aided the village dutifully and defended it honorably when it was necessary. I have received far more from these people than I have given. Their smiles of friendship have greeted me every day for fourteen years—fourteen years measured by twenty-eight unspent, unshined silver coins. And now I am free to leave to join a world I will certainly be lost in. I have a strange fear of it. The opium pipe has taken more than I care to admit.

*****

I have not been with the opium pipe for many days. Many memories have returned. I remember escorting the civilians safely from Dien Bien Phu. I did not foresee the events that have kept me here this long. I should not be considered a deserter or shirker by the Legion as I can defend my actions for every decision I was free to make. If for no other reason, I must return to make my report on the events surrounding our escape from Dien Bien Phu. I must clear my name as I can assume that it has been dishonored by my lengthy absence. It will take strength to return to the other world, but it is something I must do.

It is the day after the celebration, and I have said farewell to many. Vu and another tribesman, who has traveled to the Big River before, will be my escorts. I am glad Vu will accompany us for the journey to the settlement there. Tan and Dok wait by the longhouse as I prepare to depart. I greet Tan and thank him for my freedom. Dok looks on. He is pleased that I am leaving and does not try to conceal his happiness. Now there will be no doubt in the village as to whose power is the strongest against the phi. For Dok, the village will once again be under his control as it was before my arrival. He will have no rival. He will remain powerful in the eyes of the farmers and their families, and only Tan, the chieftain, will have more respect. Tong and Neng will remain as good omens for the village for many years to come.

Since there are very few preparations to be made, I immediately set out from the village with Vu, my aging dog Tony, and Nip, the other escort who has made the journey to the Big River village once before. The village drums begin to beat wildly. The loud drums are to frighten the evil phi back into the jungle and away from the village, where they will be unable to detect our departure. No weapons are made available to us. Our journey through the mountains again follows a maze of trails that end abruptly only to be picked up again by our guide. The deception employed in the creation of these trails has allowed the Lolo villages to remain undiscovered for countless years.

We reach the settlement on the upper reaches of the river in less than two weeks, encountering no difficulties along the way. I discover the Big River is really not big at all. At least not here! Instead, it is a rather timid mountain stream walled in on each bank by high mountain cliffs.

I am able to purchase a worn but well-made raft of heavy bamboo for one silver coin. The raft has a sturdy rudder fashioned from hardwood. Vu smiles. He believes that I have made a great bargain with the owner. He also says that he is accompanying me down the river until he can be certain of my safe return to the French. After these many years, he still remains sorrowed by my captivity. I caution my friend, saying that Tan will be upset if he does not return with Nip as expected. Vu is not swayed. He has already informed Tan of his decision to return me safely to the French. And, also unknown to me, he had conspired with Dok to have a blessing ritual performed for our protection. According to Vu, the sorcerer fell into a deep sleep during the ritual. When he woke, he said that our journey would be without harm, but only if we are careful to avoid "the mountain where no mountain should be." He is certain that these were Dok's words. Nip was already aware of Vu's decision. He leaves to return to the village immediately after purchasing two items that will bolster his standing within his clan—a rusty steering wheel from a long-abandoned truck and a brown paper box filled with angry honeybees.

With another silver coin, I am able to purchase enough provisions to last for weeks on the river with proper rationing. This same coin also buys four large metal tins and a moldy canvas tarp to protect us from the heaviest of rains. We fill the tins with fresh water from a spring nearby.

The boatman tells us to spend very little time ashore and to remain distant from all strangers. Trust no one! He speaks of pirates and bandits who would be honored to separate me from the bag of coins I carry. Be forewarned! It is very dangerous in the rapids, where the gorges narrow, and the waters become swift. These waters have tossed many travelers into the rocks, smashing their boats. Avoid the towns. There are greedy leaders in the city, and they collect tolls from those who travel on the Big River. Their laws allow them to rob you of your money. The boatman also warns us that war follows the Big River all the way to the sea. Again, be warned! The Americans are fighting Vietnamese loyalists. He says that the Americans occupy Saigon, and they run the war from there. He believes there are many French in the city. The merchant is very helpful. He predicts that our journey south should take less than two full moons, but he is not certain of this because he knows of no one who has ever returned from that great distance. We push off cautiously, aware that Tony is the only natural swimmer on the raft.

CHAPTER 32

Much has been revealed after several days on the river. The raft is a worthy craft and easily steered by using the rudder when necessary. The river moves swiftly now through deep gorges that have been cut over centuries. Although the gorges are very narrow at times, there are no boulders or other hidden dangers. It is a regrettable fact that two men and a dog are now limited to fifteen squared meters as the raft is three meters wide while five meters in length. Tony is calmer now, having adjusted well to the unsteady motion of the bouncing raft. Like all old dogs, he sleeps a lot and asks for nothing.

The boatman was right in describing this part of the river. There is no way to gauge our speed, but we are traveling very fast now, this being indicated by the rapidly passing shoreline. The raft is quiet in the swift water, and for that reason, we are able to pass very close to many hundreds of chattering monkeys and a baby elephant. We also spied two very nervous tigers. Fortunately, Tony was sleeping when we surprised the tigers, or otherwise he might have given chase. That would certainly have been the last that we would have seen of him. The days are pleasant and warm, while the nights are very cold. The canvas provides some comfort from the night's chilly air.

*****

There is no way to determine how far we have traveled in one week, but that is of little consequence. The river is slowly beginning to widen but is still no Big River. The left bank is still bounded by high mountains, while the right bank has gradually become flat as far as one can see. The flat land seems barren of man and wildlife. This contrasts greatly with the left bank, which continues to teem with an abundance of wild creatures. The river now appears to be about two hundred meters wide. We follow the advice of the boatman and keep the shore at safe distance. As the river widens, the current slackens, and so does our speed.

*****

A full moon has passed, and the Big River is finally becoming faithful to its name. The river is now about two kilometers wide, with treeless flat lands extending forever from both sides. Our pace is slow but uninterrupted. Vu and I are each stricken with the jitters because we have unwarily drifted out into the heart of the river. Even Tony seems concerned to be this far from land. We steer the raft closer to shore.

*****

Food provisions are adequate, but our supply of water will need to be replenished soon enough. The river has narrowed now to one kilometer in width, but we still continue to keep a safe distance from the left bank. The nights are no longer chilly, and the days are much hotter. A comforting breeze is always welcome. Several days of rain have allowed us to collect additional drinking water and, thus, delay our inevitable contact with strangers. During one of the storms, a fish leaped onto the raft, thus, giving Tony something to play with. Since it was the ugliest fish I had ever seen, I kicked it overboard after Tony tired of it.

We continue on, but life on the small raft has become very trying. There is little room for movement, and the handling of the rudder is our only physical activity. Occasionally, we slip off the raft to refresh ourselves in the river. When we do, we always have a very tight grip on the side. I must learn to be a better swimmer.

I worry that the cafard beetle might somehow find his way onto our boat and into my head. Long forgotten memories slowly return, now that the opium pipe no longer influences my thoughts. I think of my good friends, old Fulci and Andersen. Will I ever know what happened to my family of friends, Blackie and Guenther? I think of how I have aged and yet how I have not really grown at all. I have learned nothing that will benefit me upon my return. Once again, I willingly turn to the Legion to transform me into a worthy person. If, by chance, the Legion does not accept my explanation for these years of absence, I will have nothing but a bag of coins. If I am judged to be guilty of desertion, they will even have cause to revoke my French citizenship. Then where will I be? Then where will I go? I have only questions. I have no answers.

*****

We can no longer travel by water as the Big River has suddenly become very dangerous. An old man selling eels warns us that rebels have overthrown the government in the provinces south of us. They are executing people in large numbers. Many are being killed without reason. He says that there is no authority. A lawless state exists for the final length of our journey by water, so we will simply travel overland. Saigon, my destination all along, should be almost directly east of where we have chosen to leave the river. Who knows how long it will take us to get there? Overland will not be easy. And if we do make it to Saigon, will the French still be there?

CHAPTER 33

Vu and I have stumbled into someone else's war! We must move cautiously during the day or risk being spotted by the helos. Traveling by night is equally treacherous, but some progress is being made. Once again, Vu must resort to his wiles. We always move eastward, and so far, we have been fortunate to avoid areas that were being bombed. There does not seem to be any pattern to these barrages, either in frequency or length. Tony is frightened. It was unwise of me to bring him along. He should have remained with the Lolos. The Ami insignia was clearly visible on several of the low-flying helos earlier today. Where are the French?

*****

I am lost in the darkness of the night as I follow behind Vu. Suddenly, I am startled by the sound of a muffled explosion! Vu falls to the ground in front of me. We have entered a minefield, and the little man has stepped on an unseen mine. He grimaces in pain, yet does not cry out. I lean in to see the extent of his wounds. The blast has gaped open the flesh above Vu's right knee. The wound is deep. A shard of metal appears to be embedded in the bone. The removal of the splinter will surely require the skills of medical doctor. I am relieved to see very little bleeding from it, however. I comfort my poor friend with a sip of water and assure him that I will take care of him. Tony, frightened by the exploding mine, sits with us as we wait for first light. Only then can I determine more of our situation. We huddle with the dog for additional warmth. Nothing else can be done for now.

First light! I am not prepared for what the early morning light reveals to me. A sight to our north sends a chill throughout my body. There, rising from a perfectly flat landscape of endless rice paddies, stands a mountain of such height that its very top reaches beyond the clouds. I shudder in disbelief! This is the mountain Dok warned us of in his vision! The sorcerer was correct to warn us of this place. Harm has befallen us. Vu is badly wounded and needs the skills of a doctor. I must find a way out soon, or he will suffer more.

Now that we are in full light, I notice something else that remained unseen in the dark of night. We are not the only victims of this minefield! The bodies of two Viets in military uniforms rest where they fell several meters away. It is obvious that the soldiers have been there for a long time. I will have to make my way over to them because they may have medicine. It will be dangerous, but my friend could weaken and die if not treated soon. There are probably other mines. I will be careful.

I reach the Viets to find they were carrying two packs and two weapons when they wandered into the minefield. I try not to look at the gruesome remains. The first pack contains three rockets. I quickly set this pouch aside. The second canvas pack contains a sterile dressing bandage, a folding knife, a piece of mosquito netting and one can of mackerel. One weapon is a machine rifle, and the other is a rocket launcher. The dead Viets were probably the crew for this particular launcher. I quickly grab up the weapons and gear and retrace my steps back to Vu's side.

His eyes are fully open by now, and he, too, has seen the mountain. After cutting away the pants from Vu's injured leg, I place the clean dressing over the wound. This will keep additional dirt from getting into the open injury. Vu is fortunate because there is only a little bleeding from the wound, but this matters little because his body is weakening rapidly. His wound will become seriously infected if not treated soon. Vu continues to look with awe at the mountain where no mountain should be.

An hour has passed since first light, and I can faintly hear the sound of heavy equipment moving off in the distance. To our north, I can now see a road and a team of uniformed men and vehicles.

They appear to be clearing the road of mines. As they move nearer, it is clear that the soldiers are too large to be Vietnamese. Perhaps they are the Amis? Perhaps they control this area? And perhaps this is their minefield? If the road becomes busy, then maybe I will find an answer there? It is certain that I can do nothing if I sit here. I will move closer to the road when this detail of sappers has moved away. I must succeed, or Vu will continue to suffer. He will have to stay here with Tony. I will make him as comfortable as I possibly can and then attempt to leave the minefield in the same direction we entered from. Maybe we are only on the very edge of the minefield, and it is only a short walk to safety?

I look at the two weapons left by the dead Viets. I am not sure if the weapons will be needed in my efforts to aid Vu, but I must quickly learn how they function to benefit from their use. The automatic rifle is already loaded with a magazine. There is a safety catch above the trigger. The other weapon is a long tube for launching a rocket. There is a rocket already fully inserted in the front end of the tube. Since the Viets were carrying three additional rockets, I can assume that this launcher, unlike the Panzerfaust, is capable of firing more than one rocket. Also, unlike the Panzerfaust, the long tube does not fit under the armpit. When I attempt to do this, it is impossible to look through the sights. No, the tube must rest on the firer's shoulder to be sighted properly on the target. There is a hand-grip with a trigger and safety mounted to it. It is a very interesting weapon. I must assume that the rocket launcher is as destructive as the Panzerfaust once was. I gather up the weapons but purposely leave the additional rockets behind. There is simply no time to properly master reloading such a complicated weapon as this.

The road clearing crew has left my view, and now it is very quiet. I reposition my poor friend so that he does not face the foreboding mountain. After placing the mosquito netting over Vu to help conceal him from the helos, I command Tony to stay with Vu. I place our reserve of water within his reach, along with the recovered Viet pouch. Vu's smile encourages me as I rise to leave.

I exit the mined area as I fairly remember entering it, carefully placing a broken twig to mark my steps. I cannot relax. I can only think of the suffering my friend must endure.

I have been able to cross almost one hundred meters from where Vu rests, and I am fortunate to still be alive. There were not enough twigs to mark the last fifty meters, but it does not matter as I felt free of the minefield long before that. I move closer to the road to await traffic.

Perhaps the Amis would help if I approached them directly. Maybe they would simply mistake me for their enemy and shoot without provocation? Then Vu would certainly die!

I must decide what is necessary to save his life! I must have a plan! I must act on that plan, and it must not fail!

The plan is simple. A lone carrier with tracks is thundering toward me. If I move closer to the road, I will be in position to disable the vehicle. Vu is depending on me, and from that distance, I will have a much better chance of hitting a track. Once the vehicle has been robbed of all movement, the crew will have no choice but to evacuate their safe confines, just like the Russian tank crews in Berlin. I will then take from them that which is useful. My plan will work.

CHAPTER 34

I am very excited as I retrace my steps through the minefield with a medical kit taken from the Amis. It contains medicines to treat Vu for infection, and of course, there's morphine to relieve his suffering. He is sitting upright when I return and facing the mountain. I find that he has opened the can of mackerel for Tony. I quickly attend to his gaping wound.

I was surprised to see how young the Ami soldiers were—and they were certainly surprised to see me! Had they not been so surprised to see me, another Westerner, they may have resisted differently. The encounter was certainly to my advantage, and that is good. Had I been pressed to fire the rifle, I am not sure I could have? At that moment, I was uncertain that the vehicle actually contained anything of worth. Luck was on our side this time, and fortunately, I did not have to harm anyone.

The Amis will be looking for me now, so we will remain here in the minefield until Vu is ready to be moved. Then I will carry him out to a safer place and then return for Tony.

We must wait by the road and surrender to the Americans. They will have doctors to treat Vu, and rightfully, they should! After all, he is an innocent civilian who has been seriously injured by one of their land mines. Their doctors can halt Vu's long suffering. As for my own fate, I can only hope that I have enough silver coins to pay for the truck I crippled.

CHAPTER 35

My American captors are not brutes. They have allowed Tony to remain with me, and they have even provided him with food and water. Vu has been taken to the infirmary, where he will receive the attention he needs. I no longer worry that he will die.

My interrogation, or debriefing, as the Amis call it, is taking place in a colonel's office on a large American base. The colonel and a major have been using an interpreter for most of this day to question every detail of who I am and why I would choose to attack their men and vehicle. I tell my story, recalling events as fairly as I remember them to be. The officers seem especially interested to hear the details of the escape from Dien Bien Phu. Perhaps, they think that I am a deserter? It does not matter what the Amis believe concerning my conduct as a legionnaire. It is more important that the French believe me. I do not worry!

The translator speaks for the large American colonel. "After hearing this incredible story of yours, I'm left with a few last questions for you. This is important, so think back. When you spoke to my crew after the ambush, you said they were involved in the death of a girl. Just what did you mean by that? What girl were you speaking of?"

I listen very carefully and then respond. "I told the crew that they deserved a fate much worse than this because they were sons of the Americans who had killed my sister." I tell the story of Greta's death at the searchlight battery during the air raid that night in Berlin.

The colonel speaks again. "Well, son, I can truly understand how you must feel about losing your dear sister in such a tragic way, but you've most likely been blaming the wrong party all these years!

You see, we Americans only bombed targets during the day! The Brits flew all of the night missions! It's a fact of history!" The big colonel paused then continued. "There's another historical fact you should be aware of. World politics has changed a lot in the many years you've been in isolation. When the commies closed all the roads and trains into your hometown of Berlin, Americans kept that city and over one million people alive for a year by flying everything in from the outside. And that was no small feat either! There are many people in Germany who think highly of what we did for the Berliners!"

As I hear these words, I realize how ignorant I have become!

After the American officers agree that I could possibly be a citizen of France and entitled to the same rights as all French citizens, I am provided with clothing and passage on the next convoy to Saigon. I will be met there by officials of the French Foreign Ministry. An American military policeman is detailed to accompany me everywhere I go. Tony is also allowed to come with us.

CHAPTER 36

I am back in Saigon where my adventure began some twenty years earlier. Soon, I am taken to the personal home of an official in the French diplomatic service. Waiting there are two employees of the agency and a captain in the French Army. The younger of the two civilians says that he has been appointed as my advocate for this special inquiry. He is here to promote a measure of fair play during the hearing. He will also be allowed to participate in the inquiry with questions of his own.

The battery of questions begins. I tell my story, and again, as with the American interrogators, I tell it as I honestly remember it. There are times when I find myself struggling to remember little things, like my Legion number. But after time, even that returns to me.

"Yes, sir, I am Legionnaire Number 494321."

"Yes, sir, Third Regiment"

"Yes, sir, I was wounded in an attack on my convoy near Caobang."

"No, sir, I do not remember the year, but you may look at the bullet that struck me if you wish. I have it with me now."

"Yes, sir, corporal, First Battalion."

"Yes, sir, the Military Medal and Croix de Guerre."

"No, sir, I have no proof to verify this."

"Yes, sir, I was held captive under guard for fourteen years."

"No, sir, I would not have survived any escape. The jungle itself would have killed me."

The questions continue. The military officer asks. "How do we know that you did not desert the garrison at Dien Bien Phu before it fell to the Viets? A lot of men did, you know?"

Before answering this question, I take off the necklace which I have worn for many years. I remove the stopper from the bamboo tube and empty the contents on the table before the three men—one bullet and a piece of fabric from the Third Regimental Flag.

"Sirs, as an NCO, I was entrusted with this section of our regimental flag for safekeeping should the Viets overrun our garrison. This happened less than three days before Isabelle fell. This flag proves that I was there until the end! I am no deserter. There were many rats at Dien Bien Phu, but I was not one of them!" I sit quietly now as the captain whispers something to the other men.

"Yes! I know something about that particular flag, Corporal Koob," the captain continues. "It happened exactly as you have said. In fact, 75 percent of the flag was recovered. The surviving fragments were pieced together, and it is now displayed in the Legion Museum in France. I have seen the flag with my own eyes. You possess a marvelous piece of Legion history. And you have managed to protect it all of these years. I am sorry that I doubted this part of your story. You should be proud of this achievement!"

"Sir!" I answer, "your words have just given me hope! If 75 percent of the flag survived, then maybe 75 percent of the garrison survived as well! My friends were very determined men! They would not die so easily! You say I should be proud, when I have only obeyed a direct order."

*****

The inquiry being conducted by the French bureau has been completed. Much has been decided, and most of the news is very good. There was enough validity to my story to warrant returning me to France, where the Legion will conduct its own official hearing into my personal dilemma. There is more history to learn. The Legion Headquarters is no longer in Bel Abbes as I have always remembered it being. It has been moved from Algeria to a town in France called Aubagne.

Because of his decorated and long honorable service to the French Army, the French government has agreed to arrange transport for Vu back to the riverfront settlement on the Big River. This will happen once he has been released from the American doctors. I have been told a helo can travel there in two days. From there, he can proceed alone to join his sons in the faraway village. Someday, if he is wise, he may take another wife. I will never see the little montagnard again, but I am at peace knowing that he is being treated well. He will have much to tell the villagers of Dok's visions upon his return. Our many debts, imagined or real, will be paid at last

I was informed that Tony could travel to France with me if I was willing to pay his fare. He is worth the silver coin it cost for his ticket. According to my advocate, my personal worth will be dictated by the Legion only after its full inquiry has been completed. The advocate says that he will lobby for ration pay during my years of captivity. The Legion might be opposed to this idea since they assume that prisoners of war are fed by their captors. However, the French government might be embarrassed if it were widely known that they were in violation of the Geneva Accords. These accords prohibit the presence of French soldiers anywhere in Indochina, and I am, at heart, still a French soldier! Ration pay for twelve years could be several hundred thousand francs. The advocate says that I must be patient and address the Legion's inquiry board first. There may be an additional sum of money in back pay if I am vindicated completely. That could be an even larger sum of money! The advocate warns that I should be aware that newsmen from several countries have requested interviews with me. It seems that my sudden arrival at the American Army base had created significant interest among a few idle war reporters. He says that my adventure is considered to be very interesting to many people. After all, there were only a few who managed to escape from Dien Bien Phu and were able to avoid captivity. The advocate says that the American journalists would pay me in American dollars if I sold them the story of our escape into the mountains.

What was my reward for this successful and daring escape—fourteen years of captivity? I was young, healthy, and free of wounds or injury. I was cursed by those orders! I could have fought beside my comrades instead of struggling blindly through those hellish mountains. I was strong enough to survive the conditions of any prison of war by any captor! That escape proved to be a mistake that I paid for with over fourteen years of my life!

The Americans have agreed to permit my travel to France. They have also recalled the MP sergeant. The older of the two French agency workers has a room for guests behind his quarters. He has invited Tony and I to stay here as we are not presently needed. There are towels and hot water and clean sheets on a soft bed. Before today, I would have thought these things could only be found in a hospital room. My advocate has exchanged my remaining silver coins for francs. These will be transferred to a bank in France. He has also purchased a travel bag and new clothing for the journey. I will always be grateful for these acts of kindness.

Today, my advocate has news of the beautiful Hanh Long! She arrived safely after all. That is very good news. She made an official report to the current French administration when she returned, but it was not investigated further. The French were in the process of abandoning all of Indochina at the time, and chaos ruled. He says he learned that she is now married to a physician from Hong Kong, where they now live. That is all the information he was able to find through his bureau. I am excited to hear this!

CHAPTER 37

Tony and I complete our flight from Saigon to Paris, but upon leaving the plane, we immediately find ourselves being spooked by the many bright unnecessary lights everywhere. Swarms of excited people rush hurriedly by in the confusing terminal. The urge to panic is overwhelming. Tony, wearing a collar and leash for the first time in his old life, feels as I do—lost! After a very short time, however, we are met by two airport policemen who escort us to a waiting bus for the ride to Aubagne.

It is dark and beginning to rain as we arrive at the Legion Headquarters. I am taken directly to the post hospital where I am subjected to a thorough physical examination. I am tired but thankful to finally be here.

I experience a restless night before being escorted to my hearing. I arrive to find that the Legion has wasted no time preparing for this inquiry. They have already selected three senior officers and two NCOs to be seated on the board. I understand that two members of the board were present at Dien Bien Phu. It is important that their recollections of events there parallel my own. That would certainly be to my advantage. I do not have a uniform, and even if I did, I would not be allowed to wear it to this hearing. Instead, I have been presented with a clean starched khaki blouse, a brown belt, and khaki pants. Unless this board vindicates me completely, I will never wear the Legion uniform again!

The presiding officer calls the board to order. He introduces himself and the other respective members of the inquiry board, asking each if they have had enough time to study their copy of my Legion Service Record. After each member has acknowledged affirmatively to this question, I am once again asked to recall the events which have brought me here today. I do this without interruption, knowing the panels' questions will be coming only after I have been given the opportunity to account for fourteen years of unauthorized absence. This is the greatest challenge I will ever face, so I must be bold—as bold as the boy who lied about his age to join the Legion! I must never look down as I testify but directly into the faces of my judges. Although I should feel intimidated by these men in their immaculate uniforms, I do not. I tell my story!

"Yes, sir, I was fifteen years old, but I would soon be sixteen."

"No, sir, I do not know the rank or name of the injured pilot."

"No, sir, I did not volunteer to lead the civilians to safety. It came as an order from the battalion."

"No, sir, we did not have a compass."

"Yes, sir, I have treated many types of wounds."

"Yes, sir, it was the only way I could rejoin my friends in the battalion."

"Yes, sir, I would gladly do it again tomorrow…and for the same reason."

"No, sir, I have never been disciplined as a legionnaire."

"Yes, sir, my freedom was returned suddenly—as an unexpected gift. I was a dead man! I would have languished there forever!"

The questions are very similar to those asked by the officials in Saigon. The hearing is halted for soupe and then continues. Eventually, I am asked to produce my share of the Third Regimental Flag, which I carefully place on a small wooden tray. The relic is passed to each member for closer examination and then is positioned in front of the presiding officer. It is allowed to remain there. I sense that I have touched something familiar and dear for the last time. It will not be returned to me but will go directly to the museum, where it will be reunited with the other mutilated survivors.

As the inquiry draws to an end for the day, I feel I have defended my actions well. I am pleased to learn that I will not be placed under guard. However, I am instructed not to leave the post for any reason. They do not know that I would never leave anyway. I want to be here! Although this place is different and completely unfamiliar to me, it feels like I belong here. Eagerly, I return to my assigned quarters to find Tony excited to see me. It is good to be away from all the questions until the board resumes tomorrow. I rest with my dog.

At first, I am made aware of laughter and loud voices just outside my quarters. Fists pound hard against my door. Tony is frightened, so he wisely backs away into another room. Someone outside is saying, "Will you open this door or not?" I open the door!

Two men stand together on the sidewalk under the weak glow of a streetlight. They are laughing as if they have just left a great wild party. As they come nearer to give better view of their smiling faces, I recognize them to be lost friends—Blackie, still with his gold tooth, and Guenther, with his arms of steel! I have no words to express my feelings at the sight of seeing them here safe and well! My last prayer was answered after all!

My friends have much to talk about. Guenther has married. He even has a son! Guenther is a civilian now, but he works on post at the Legion newspaper. It is fitting that the Legion newspaper would be called *Kepi Blanc*! He is a supervisor in the printing department. He was at work when the news of a long-lost legionnaire's arrival in Saigon caught his eye. As the story grew in detail, Guenther began to be encouraged that I might be the missing survivor. He says he did not have to wait long because my identity was soon disclosed on the American television news. He then rushed to share this good news with Blackie and Sergent Andersen.

Yes! Of course! Sergent Andersen is alive and well!

Blackie agrees to tell Andersen's tale for him since the old sergent has retired from the Legion. He lives in the Legion's retirement community in the town of Puyloubier. It is nearby, only a short drive from here. The wine there is excellent. We will visit him at the first opportunity, maybe even tomorrow? Blackie continues on. The retirement home is a busy place for the disabled veterans. They have workshops where they make and sell crafts. Many of the old vets have interesting hobbies. Andersen, himself, has become very skilled at engraving headstones for other retirees. He works the stones beautifully. They are the true passion in his life. He has been renewed. Even his hygiene problem has disappeared! Guenther and Blackie were told in private that the other residents insist that the old Swede bathe weekly. We all laugh at this! What a life Andersen is now having! He is always working and always cheerful to be around. Joyous news of a lost old friend!

Blackie has been promoted to sergent-chef in our old regiment. He remains an unmarried lover of all women. He, too, is happy with his good fortune. I am greatly saddened to hear of dear old Fulci and his death three weeks after being taken prisoner by the Viets. His malaria-ridden body was just too weak to survive the primitive conditions of their prison camp. He died peacefully enough, knowing that Andersen, Guenther, and Blackie were there to bury him. I will always remember three things about Cabo Fulci, the old Legion muleskinner. I remember his generous nature and his loyalty to his embattled comrades, even if it meant jumping from an airplane at night to join them. And I remember his special wish—to have a few true friends to mourn his passing! Corporal Fulci could not have found truer friends!

Guenther wishes to continue with their story. Solemnly, he tells of being held captive long enough to see hundreds of their comrades die of disease. Hundreds more died from the infections of their untreated wounds. Many suffered horribly before dying in the inhumane conditions. As Blackie says, "Only hell itself could accommodate more human misery." After being released from the prison camp, the surviving legionnaires were quickly returned to Algeria

They returned, only to discover that Algerian rebels had started a movement to free the country from French control. After the separatists had killed many innocent people by exploding bombs in public places, the French government granted Algeria its independence. When this happened, many high-ranking Legion officers refused to accept it. Their attempted military coup was smashed, and they were arrested. Some of those involved were tried and dishonored. Others were acquitted. Guenther quickly explains that neither he nor Blackie were stupid enough to fight against France. They were involved, however, in the relocation of Legion Headquarters from Sidi Bel Abbes to its present location in France. Everything was moved except for the buildings themselves. They were even witnesses to the removal of the grand Monumente de Morte from Bel Abbes.

It must have been heartbreaking for many of the old soldiers when ordered out of Algeria. It must have been a sad time. Guenther says that, today, there are only a few old legionnaires around here who even remember the old post in Bel Abbes. The veterans are scattered all over, but they always manage to return for the celebration of the Camerone each year. We laugh in surprise as Tony wanders into the room to join us.

Our spirited reunion lasts well into the early morning. I have never wanted to talk this much before tonight. My excited friends have answered many questions this night, but the morning brings with it responsibilities for each of us. They will need to report to their regular duties, and I will need to address the board of inquiry for the second time. My friends leave after we agree to meet here later today. I am alone now, and happy. My mind is finally at peace.

CHAPTER 38

After a round of questions from the panel of officers, I am released with instructions to return in the morning. This second day of hearings has ended surprisingly early, and I am not sure of the reason. Perhaps, it is in my favor?

I am left alone to stroll the unfamiliar grounds of the new Headquarters. I easily find the Legion museum with its relocated relics and exhibits. I enter, and as before over twenty years earlier, I am filled with awe at the sight of these many treasures. I move through the regimental histories and find a collection of flags being proudly displayed in glass cabinets. There before me is the regiment's flag from Dien Bien Phu! It has been quilted together from the pieces that survived capture by the Viets. I sadly conclude that the missing pieces must have been carried by legionnaires who did not survive the campaign. I look closely. There! I see it! I see the exact spot where my piece will be added. Yes! That is certainly where it belongs! Yes! I do feel proud of myself!

It is a short walk to the Monumente de Morte. It stands as I remember it, a somber memorial to those who died under a Legion flag. I cannot remember the name of the friendly Pole from the garrison at Phu Tong Hoa, but I do remember his face and his sacrifice for the regiment. This memorial is for him...and for old Fulci. I return to my quarters to rest with Tony until my friends arrive. I have not slept in days.

I am awakened by a soft knock on the door. My friends have arrived. Guenther speaks first. "Well, Dieter, I must tell you that you have become quite a famous character. The press continues to focus on your situation. Even now, they are clamoring to uncover every little detail of your life. People love to read and hear about true-life adventures, and currently, yours is the most interesting one available. Even I think it is incredible! What do you think of all that?"

I do think about what Guenther says. Being famous matters little. Hitler was famous, and so was Tom Mix. Their fame destroyed them. Five strangers will soon decide my fate. This matters more.

Blackie smiles silently from across the room. He removes one of the bottles of wine from a bag he carries. He opens the bottle and passes it to me. "This wine is from the vineyards at Puyloubier. It is very good, however, I do not need to tell you. You will discover that for yourself. Drink! We still have much to talk about!"

*****

The hearing of the third day begins with presiding officer announcing that the board of inquiry has no need for any further testimony or deliberation. They have reached a judgment at last! He motions for me to rise and stand before him.

The colonel begins. "The purpose for this inquiry has been to determine if there was enough sufficient evidence to remand you for court martial on a single charge of desertion. After reviewing your service record and all of the testimony obtained from this hearing as well as copies of testimony taken from the inquiry by officials of the French Diplomacy Bureau in Saigon, the members of this board have determined that your extended absence from Legion service resulted from your personal confinement by forces considered to be hostile to the Laotian government."

I am greatly relieved upon hearing this! The doubt and uncertainty has been removed at last!

The colonel continues. "This board of inquiry has also determined that your conduct has been honorable during this absence. As a result, the board is recommending that you be fully reintegrated back into Legion service immediately, with restoration of your former rank of corporal. The accounting department will be notified to provide you with an assessment of financial entitlements or afforded benefits commensurate with the rank of corporal. The Legion will provide you with the resources necessary for your complete rehabilitation." The colonel pauses very briefly and then concludes by saying, "Corporal Dieter Koob, the members of this board are unanimous in welcoming you back to the Legion!"

CHAPTER 39

Guenther arrives at my quarters. He has brought food. He says that I am very lucky to have a friend working at the newspaper. And it is true! Guenther has more news of concern to me. He says that a ceremony is being planned for me to finally receive the medals that were awarded in 1954. He says that arrangements are being made for the medals to be presented to me by the Navy pilot whose life I saved. Guenther says that the pilot is now a Lieutenant Commander in the French Navy. I remind Guenther that Vu was with me that day, and he was equally responsible for the successful rescue of the Navy flyer. I am happy to learn that the pilot was able to survive his confinement and eventually recover from his many injuries. All the news is good today!

Tony is suddenly startled by a knock at the door. There, alongside Blackie, is an old fellow who stands with the support of a single crutch. It can only be Sergent Andersen! He is smiling and obviously glad to be reunited with the veterans of Bel Abbes. And what joy it is to see him!

The old veteran finally speaks. "God has delivered you safely back to where you truly belong, Cabo Koob, and those of us here today will help you as you begin your new life. It is a glorious day! Welcome *home!*"

END

GLOSSARY

APC—U.S. armored personnel carrier (M113), Also referred to as "tracks" or "tracs". They offered only light armor protection for crews and passengers.

TC—Track (APC) commander

Laager—temporary defensive position

Dakota—adopted French nickname for the DC-3 or C-47 military transport plane

Vinogel—wine-like beverage made by adding water to dehydrated wine crystals

Day of Camerone—April 30, 1863—considered to be the most defining military engagement in Legion history. Although greatly out-numbered by the Mexican army, a detachment of sixty-five legionnaires fought valiantly refusing to surrender until all were either killed or wounded. Their sacrifice is remembered every year on this special day.

Sappers—engineers of the French Colonial forces

PK—Poste kilometers—numbered stone location markers on French Colonial routes

Big River—MeKong River

ABOUT THE AUTHOR

Alexander Malone is a veteran with military service in Vietnam. He became especially interested in the folklore of that conflict. Of all the tales, myths, and stories, he was always attracted to the rumor of the lone Caucasian warrior who supposedly lived and fought along-side the Viet Cong. He was always referred to as the White Cong.

Malone was intrigued by this particular character. How could this be? The more he speculated about the character's motivation, the more he was convinced to give "life" to his very own "White Cong."

Malone was also fascinated early in life by the mystique of the French Foreign Legion. As a preteen, the young newspaper carrier would watch the evening TV news anxiously with his family for the frequent reports coming from French Indochina on the lengthy siege of Dien Bien Phu. The legionnaires, fighting there with the French Colonial forces, were overwhelmingly outnumbered by the communist Viet Minh forces, yet defeat seemed to be an improbability.

What an exciting adventure for a kid to follow in the city news-paper and the national TV news. *The Deliverance of Cabo Koob...*an exciting escape to an exciting time!

CPSIA information can be obtained
at www.ICGtesting.com
Printed in the USA
LVHW092201140721
692588LV00018B/731